The Amazing Marriage

Volume 4

by

George Meredith

Double 9 BOOKS

The Amazing Marriage

Volume 4

by George Meredith

ISBN: 978-93-74833-86-5

Published by

DOUBLE 9 BOOKS

2/13-B, Ansari Road
Daryaganj, New Delhi – 110002
info@double9books.com
www.double9books.com
Tel. 011-40042856

ABOUT THE AUTHOR

George Meredith was an English novelist and poet, born on February 12, 1828. Meredith was born to Thomas Meredith and Jane Cholmeley. He was a prominent figure in the Victorian era, initially known for his poetry, which was heavily influenced by poets like John Keats. Over time, Meredith transitioned into novel writing and became recognized for his works in this genre. His novel The Ordeal of Richard Feverel (1859) caused a stir in Victorian literary circles due to its controversial themes. However, it was his later novels, such as The Egoist (1879) and Diana of the Crossways (1885) that earned him enduring acclaim. His works often explored complex psychological and moral dilemmas, blending wit with serious social critique. Meredith's other notable works include The Shaving of Shagpat (1856), Farina (1857), and Evan Harrington (1861). Throughout his career, he developed a reputation for his intricate character studies and exploration of human nature. Meredith's influence extended well into the 20th century, and his work remains a key part of Victorian literature.

CONTENTS

BOOK 4

CHAPTER XXIX
CARINTHIA IN WALES

An August of gales and rains drove Atlantic air over the Welsh highlands. Carinthia's old father had impressed on her the rapture of 'smelling salt' when by chance he stood and threw up his nostrils to sniff largely over a bed of bracken, that reminded him of his element, and her fancy would be at strain to catch his once proud riding of the seas. She felt herself an elder daughter of the beloved old father, as she breathed it in full volume from the billowy West one morning early after sunrise and walked sisterly with the far-seen inexperienced little maid, whom she saw trotting beside him through the mountain forest, listening, storing his words, picturing the magnetic, veined great gloom of an untasted world.

This elder daughter had undergone a shipwreck; but clear proof that she had not been worsted was in the unclouded liveliness of the younger one gazing forward. Imaginative creatures who are courageous will never be lopped of the hopeful portion of their days by personal misfortune. Carinthia could animate both; it would have been a hurt done to a living human soul had she suffered the younger self to run overcast. Only, the gazing forward had become interdicted to her experienced self. Nor could she vision a future having any horizon for her child. She saw it in bleak squares, and snuggled him between dangers weathered and dangers apprehended.

The conviction that her husband hated her had sunk into her nature. Hating the mother, he would not love her boy. He was her boy, and strangely bestowed, not beautifully to be remembered rapturously or gratefully, and with deep love of the father. She felt the wound recollection dealt her. But the boy was her one treasure, and no treasure to her husband. They were burdens, and the heir of his House, child of a hated mother, was under perpetual menace from an unscrupulous tyrannical man. The dread and antagonism were first aroused by the birth of her child. She had not known while bearing him her present acute sensation of the hunted flying and at bay. Previously, she could say: I did wrong here; I did wrong there. Distrust had brought the state of war, which allows not of the wasting of our powers in confessions.

Her husband fed her and he clothed her; the limitation of his bounty was sharply outlined. Sure of her rectitude, a stranger to the world, she was not very sensible of dishonour done to her name. It happened at times that her father inquired of her how things were going with his little Carin; and then revolt sprang up and answered on his behalf rather fiercely. She was, however, prepared for any treaty including forgiveness, if she could be at peace in regard to her boy, and have an income of some help to her brother. Chillon was harassed on all sides; she stood incapable of aiding; so foolishly feeble in the shadow of her immense longing to strive for him, that she could think her husband had purposely lamed her with an infant. Her love of her brother, now the one man she loved, laid her insufficiency on the rack and tortured imbecile cries from it.

On the contrary, her strange husband had blest her with an infant. Everything was pardonable to him if he left her boy untouched in the mother's charge. Much alone as she was, she raised the dead to pet and cherish her boy. Chillon had seen him and praised him. Mrs. Owain Wythan, her neighbour over a hill, praised him above all babes on earth, poor childless woman!

She was about to cross the hill and breakfast with Mrs. Wythan. The time for the weaning of the babe approached, and had as prospect beyond it her dull fear that her husband would say the mother's work was done, and seize the pretext to separate them: and she could not claim a longer term to be giving milk, because her father had said: 'Not a quarter of a month more than nine for the milk of the mother'—or else the child would draw an unsustaining nourishment from the strongest breast. She could have argued her exceptional robustness against another than he. But the dead father wanting to build a great race of men and women ruled.

Carinthia knelt at the cradle of a princeling gone from the rich repast to his alternative kingdom.

'You will bring him over when he wakes,' she said to Madge. 'Mrs. Wythan would like to see him every day. Martha can walk now.'

'She can walk and hold a child in her two arms, my lady,' said Madge. 'She expects miners popping up out of the bare ground when she sees no goblins.'

'They!—they know him, they would not hurt him, they know my son,' her mistress answered.

The population of the mines in revolt had no alarms for her. The works were empty down below. Men sat by the wayside brooding or strolled in groups, now and then loudly exercising their tongues; or they stood in circle to sing hymns: melancholy chants of a melancholy time for all.

How would her father have acted by these men? He would have been among them. Dissensions in his mine were vapours of a day. Lords behaved differently. Carinthia fancied the people must regard their master as a foreign wizard, whose power they felt, without the chance of making their cry to him heard. She, too, dealt with a lord. It was now his wish for her to leave the place where she had found some shreds of a home in the thought of being useful. She was gathering the people's language; many of their songs she could sing, and please them by singing to them. They were not suspicious of her; at least, their women had open doors for her; the men, if shy, were civil. She had only to go below, she was greeted in the quick tones of their speech all along the street of the slate- roofs.

But none loved the castle, and she as little, saving the one room in it where her boy lay. The grey of Welsh history knew a real castle beside the roaring brook frequently a torrent. This was an eighteenth century castellated habitation on the verge of a small wood midway up the height, and it required a survey of numberless happy recollections to illumine its walls or drape its chambers. The permanently lighted hearth of a dear home, as in that forsaken unfavoured old white house of the wooded Austrian crags, it had not. Rather it seemed a place waiting for an ill deed to be done in it and stop all lighting of hearths thereafter.

Out on the turf of the shaven hills, her springy step dispersed any misty fancies. Her short-winged hive set to work in her head as usual, building scaffoldings of great things to be done by Chillon, present evils escaped. The rolling big bade hills with the riding clouds excited her as she mounted, and she was a figure of gladness on the ridge bending over to hospitable Plas Llwyn, where the Wythans lived, entertaining rich and poor alike.

They had led the neighbourhood to call on the discarded
Countess of Fleetwood.

A warm strain of arms about her neck was Carinthia's welcome from Mrs. Wythan lying along the couch in her boudoir; an established invalid, who yearned sanely to life, and caught a spark of it from the guest eyed tenderly by her as they conversed.

'Our boy?—our Chillon Kirby till he has his baptism
names; he is well?
I am to see him?'

'He follows me. He sleeps almost through the night now.'

'Ah, my dear,' Mrs. Wythan sighed, imagining: 'It would disappoint me if he did not wake me.'

'I wake at his old time and watch him.'

Carinthia put on the baby's face in the soft mould of slumber.

'I see him!' Mrs. Wythan cried. 'He is part mine. He has taught Owain to love babies.'

A tray of breakfast was placed before the countess. 'Mr. Wythan is down among his men?' she said.

'Every morning, as long as this agitation lasts. I need not say good appetite to you after your walk. You have no fear of the men, I know. Owain's men are undisturbed; he has them in hand. Absentee masters can't expect continued harmony. Dear, he tells me Mr. Edwards awaits the earl.'

Drinking her tea, Carinthia's eyelids shut; she set down her cup, 'If he must come,' she said. 'He wishes me to leave. I am to go again where I have no friends, and no language to learn, and can be of no use. It is not for me that I dread his coming. He speaks to command. The men ask to be heard. He will have submission first. They do not trust him. His coming is a danger. For me, I should wish him to come. May I say . . ?'

'Your Rebecca bids you say, my darling.'

'It is, I am with the men because I am so like them. I beg to be heard. He commands obedience. He is a great nobleman, but I am the daughter of a greater man, and I have to say, that if those poor miners do harm, I will not stand by and see an anger against injustice punished. I wish his coming, for him to agree upon the Christian names of the boy. I feel his coming will do me, injury in making me offend him worse. I would avoid that. Oh, dear soul! I may say it to you:—he cannot hurt me any more. I am spared loving him when I forgive him; and I do. The loving is the pain. That is gone by.'

Mrs. Wythan fondled and kissed Carinthia's hand.

'Let me say in my turn; I may help you, dear. You know I have my husband's love, as he mine. Am I, have I ever been a wife to him? Here I lie, a dead weight, to be carried up and down, all of a wife that Owain has had for years. I lie and pray to be taken, that my good man, my proved good man, may be free to choose a healthy young woman and be rewarded before his end by learning what a true marriage is. The big simpleton will otherwise be going to his grave, thinking he was married! I see him stepping about softly in my room, so contented if he does not disturb me, and he crushes me with a desire to laugh at him while I worship. I tricked him into marrying the prostrate invalid I am, and he can't discover the trick, he will think it's a wife he has, instead of a doctor's doll. Oh! you have a strange husband, it has been a strange marriage for you, but you have your invincible health, you have not to lie and feel the horror of being a deception to a guileless man, whose love blindfolds him. The bitter ache to me is, that I can give nothing. You abound in power to give.'

Carinthia lifted her open hands for sign of their emptiness.

'My brother would not want, if I could give. He may have to sell out of. the army, he thinks, fears; and I must look on. Our mother used to say she had done something for her country in giving a son like Chillon to the British army. Poor mother! Our bright opening days all seem to end in rain. We should turn to Mr. Wythan for a guide.'

'He calls you Morgan le Fay christianized.'

'What I am!' Carinthia raised and let fall her head. 'An example makes dwarfs of us. When Mr. Wythan does penance for temper by descending into his mine and working among his men for a day with the pick, seated, as he showed me down below, that is an example. If I did like that, I should have no firedamp in the breast, and not such a task to forgive, that when I succeed I kill my feelings.'

The entry of Madge and Martha, the nurse-girl, with the overflowing armful of baby, changed their converse into melodious exclamations.

'Kit Ines has arrived, my lady,' Madge said. 'I saw him on the road and stopped a minute.'

Mrs. Wythan studied Carinthia. Her sharp invalid's ears had caught the name. She beckoned. 'The man who—the fighting man?'

'It will be my child this time,' said Carinthia; 'I have no fear for myself.' She was trembling, though her features were hard for the war her lord had declared, as it seemed. 'Did he tell you his business here?' she asked of Madge.

'He says, to protect you, my lady, since you won't leave.'

'He stays at the castle?'

'He is to stay there, he says, as long as the Welsh are out.'

'The "Welsh" are misunderstood by Lord Fleetwood,'

Mrs. Wythan said to Carinthia. 'He should live among them. They will not hurt their lady. Protecting may be his intention; but we will have our baby safe here. Not?' she appealed. 'And baby's mother. How otherwise?'

'You read my wishes,' Carinthia rejoined. 'The man I do not think a bad man. He has a master. While I am bound to my child I must be restful, and with the man at the castle Martha's goblins would jump about me day and night. My boy makes a coward of his mother.'

'We merely take a precaution, and I have the pleasure of it,' said her hostess. 'Give orders to your maid not less than a fortnight. It will rejoice my husband so much.'

As with the warmly hospitable, few were the words. Madge was promised by her mistress plenty of opportunities daily for seeing Kit Ines, and her mouth screwed to one of women's dimples at a corner. She went off in a cart to fetch boxes, thinking: We are a hunted lot! So she was not mildly disposed for the company of Mr. Kit on her return to the castle.

England's champion light-weight thought it hard that his, coming down to protect the castle against the gibbering heathen Welsh should cause a clearing out, and solitariness for his portion.

'What's the good of innocence if you 're always going to suspect a man!' he put it, like a true son of the pirates turned traders. 'I've got a paytron, and a man in my profession must have a paytron, or where is he? Where's his money for a trial of skill? Say he saves and borrows and finds the lump to clap it down, and he's knocked out o' time. There he is, bankrup', and a devil of a licking into the bargain. That 's the cream of our profession, if a man has got no paytron.

No prize-ring can live without one. The odds are too hard on us. My lady ought to take into account I behaved respectful when I was obliged to do my lord's orders and remove her from our haunts, which wasn't to his taste. Here I'm like a cannon for defending the house, needs be, and all inside flies off scarified.'

'It strikes me, Kit Ines, a man with a paytron is no better than a tool of a man,' said Madge.

'And don't you go to be sneering at honest tools,' Ines retorted. 'When will women learn a bit of the world before they're made hags of by old Father Wear-and-Tear! A young woman in her prime, you Madge! be such a fool as not see I serve tool to stock our shop.'

'Your paytron bid you steal off with my lady's child, Kit Ines, you'd do it to stock your shop.'

Ines puffed. 'If you ain't a girl to wallop the wind! Fancy me at that game! Is that why my lady—but I can't be suspected that far? You make me break out at my pores. My paytron's a gentleman: he wouldn't ask and I couldn't act such a part. Dear Lord! it'd have to be stealing off, for my lady can use a stick; and put it to the choice between my lady and her child and any paytron living, paytron be damned, I'd say, rather'n go against my notions of honour. Have you forgot all our old talk about the prize-ring, the nursery of honour in Old England?'

'That was before you sold yourself to a paytron, Kit Ines.'

'Ah! Women wants mast-heading off and on, for 'em to have a bit of a look-out over life as it is. They go stewing over books of adventure and drop into frights about awful man. Take me, now; you had a no small admiration for my manly valour once, and you trusted yourself to me, and did you ever repent it?—owning you're not the young woman to tempt to t' other way.'

'You wouldn't have found me talking to you here if I had.'

'And here I'm left to defend an empty castle, am I?'

'Don't drink or you'll have your paytron on you. He's good use there.'

'I ask it, can I see my lady?'

'Drunk nor sober you won't. Serve a paytron, be a leper, you'll find, with all honest folk.'

Ines shook out an execrating leg at the foul word. 'Leper, you say? You say that? You say leper to me?'

'Strut your tallest, Kit Ines. It's the money rattles in your pocket says it.'

'It's my reputation for decent treatment of a woman lets
you say it,
Madge Winch.'

'Stick to that as long as your paytron consents. It's the one thing you've got left.'

'Benefit, you hussy, and mind you don't pull too stiff.'

'Be the woman and have the last word!'

His tongue was checked. He swallowed the exceeding sourness of a retort undelivered, together with the feeling that she beat him in the wrangle by dint of her being an unreasonable wench.

Madge huffed away to fill her boxes.

He stood by the cart, hands deep down his pockets, when she descended. She could have laughed at the spectacle of a champion prize-fighter out of employ, hulking idle, because he was dog to a paytron; but her contempt of him declined passing in small change.

'So you're off. What am I to tell my lord when he
comes?' Kit growled.
'His yacht's fetching for a Welsh seaport.'

She counted it a piece of information gained, and jumped to her seat, bidding the driver start. To have pretty well lost her character for a hero changed into a patron's dog, was a thought that outweighed the show of incivility. Some little distance away, she reproached herself for not having been so civil as to inquire what day my lord was expected, by his appointment. The girl reflected on the strangeness of a body of discontented miners bringing my lord and my lady close, perhaps to meet.

CHAPTER XXX
REBECCA WYTHAN

The earl was looked for at the, chief office of the mines, and each day an expectation of him closed in disappointment, leaving it to be surmised that there were more serious reasons for his continued absence during a crisis than any discussed; whether indeed, as when a timepiece neglects to strike the hour which is, by the reckoning of natural impatience, past, the capital charge of 'crazy works' must not be brought against a nobleman hitherto precise upon business, of a just disposition, fairly humane. For though he was an absentee sucking the earth through a tube, in Ottoman ease, he had never omitted the duty of personally attending on the spot to grave cases under dispute. The son of the hardheaded father came out at a crisis; and not too highhandedly: he could hear an opposite argument to the end. Therefore, since he refused to comply without hearing, he was wanted on the spot imperatively, now.

Irony perusing History offers the beaten and indolent a sugary acid in the indication of the spites and the pranks, the whims and the tastes, at the springs of main events. It is, taken by itself, destructive nourishment. But those who labour in the field to shovel the clods of earth to History, would be wiser of their fellows for a minor dose of it. Mr. Howell Edwards consulting with Mr. Owain Wythan on the necessity, that the earl should instantly keep his promise to appear among the men and stop the fermentation, as in our younger days a lordly owner still might do by small concessions and the physical influence—the nerve- charm—could suppose him to be holding aloof for his pleasure or his pride; perhaps because of illness or inability to conceive the actual situation at a distance. He mentioned the presence of the countess, and Mr. Wythan mentioned it, neither of them thinking a rational man would so play the lunatic as to let men starve, and wreck precious mines, for the sake of avoiding her.

Sullen days went by. On these days of the slate-cloud or the leaden-winged, Carinthia walked over the hills to her staring or down eyed silent people, admitted without a welcome at some doors, rejected at some. Her baskets from the castle were for the most part received as graciously. She continued to direct them for delivery where they were needed, and understood why a charity that supplied the place of justice was not thanked.

She and her people here were one regarding the master, as she had said. They could not hurt her sensitiveness, she felt too warmly with them. And here it was not the squalid, flat, bricked east- corner of London at the close of her daily pilgrimage. Up from the solitary street of the slate-roofs, she mounted a big hill and had the life of high breathing. A perpetual escape out of the smoky, grimy city mazes was trumpeted to her in the winds up there: a recollected contrast lightened the skyless broad spaces overhead almost to sunniness. Having air of the hills and activity for her limbs, she made sunshine for herself. Regrets were at no time her nestlings.

Look backward only to correct an error of conduct for the next attempt, says one of her father's Maxims; as sharply bracing for women as for men. She did not look back to moan. Now that her hunger for the safety of her infant was momentarily quieted, she could see Kit Ines hanging about the lower ground, near the alehouse, and smile at Madge's comparison of him to a drummed-out soldier, who would like to be taken for a holiday pensioner.

He saluted; under the suspicion of his patron's lady his legs were hampered, he dared not approach her; though his innocence of a deed not proposed to him yet—and all to stock that girl Madge's shop, if done! knocked at his ribs with fury to vindicate himself before the lady and her maid. A gentleman met them and conducted them across the hills.

And two Taffy gentlemen would hardly be sufficient for the purpose, supposing an ill-used Englishman inclined to block their way!—What, and play footpad, Kit Ines? No, it's just a game in the head. But a true man hates to feel himself suspected. His refuge is the beer of the country.

Next day there were the two gentlemen to conduct the lady and her maid; and Taffy the first walks beside the countess; and that girl Madge trudges along with no other than my lord's Mr. Woodseer, chattering like a watering-can on a garden-bed: deuce a glance at Kit Ines. How can she keep it up and the gentleman no more than nodding? How does he enjoy playing second fiddle with the maid while Mr. tall brown-face Taffy violins it to her ladyship a stone's throw in front? Ines had less curiosity to know the object of Mr. Woodseer's appearance on the scene. Idle, unhandsomely treated, and a cave of the yawns, he merely commented on his observations.

'Yes, there he is, don't look at him,' Madge said to Gower; 'and whatever he's here for, he has a bad time of it, and rather more than it's pleasant for him to think over, if a slave to a "paytron" thinks at all. I won't judge him; my mistress is bitten with the fear for the child, worse than ever. And the earl, my lord, not coming, and he wanting her to move again, seems to her he durstn't do it here and intends to snap at the child on the road. She-'s forced to believe anything of such a husband and father. And why does he behave so? I can't spell it. He's kind to my Sally—you've seen the Piccadilly shop?—because she was . . . she did her best in love and duty for my lady. And behaves like a husband hating his wife's life on earth! Then he went down with good Mr. Woodseer, and called on Sally, pretending to inquire, after she was kidnapped by that Kit Ines acting to please his paytron, he must be shown up to the room where she slept, and stands at the door and peeps in, Sally's letter says, and asks if he may enter the room. He went to the window looking on the chimneys she used to see, and touched an ornament over the fireplace, called grandfather's pigtail case—he was a sailor; only a ridiculous piece of china, that made my lady laugh about the story of its holding a pigtail. But he turns it over because she did—Sally told him. He couldn't be pretending when he bought the beautiful shop and stocked it for Sally. He gets her lots of customers; and no rent to pay till next Michaelmas a year. She's a made woman through him. He said to her, he had heard from Mr. Woodseer the Countess of Fleetwood called her sister; he shook her hand.'

'The Countess of Fleetwood called both of you her sisters,
I think,' said Gower.

'I'm her servant. I'd rather serve her than have a fortune.'

'You were born with a fortune one would like to have a nibble at, Madge.'

'I can't lay hand on it, then.'

'It's the capacity for giving, my dear.'

'Please, Mr. Gower, don't say that; you'll make me cry. He keeps his wife so poor she hasn't a shilling of her own; she wearies about her brother; she can't help. He can spend hundreds on my Sally for having been good to her, in our small way—it's a fairy tale; and he won't hear of money for his wife, except that she's never to want for anything it can buy.'

'You give what it can't buy.'

'Me. I'm "a pugilist's wench"—I've heard myself called. She was the first who gave me a lift; never mind me. Have you come to take her away? She'd trust herself and the child to you.'

'Take her?—reason with her as to the best we can do. He holds off from a meeting just now. I fancy he's wearing round to it. His keeping his wife without money passes comprehension. After serving him for a few months, I had a store invested to support me for years—as much as I need before I join the ranks of the pen. I was at my reading and writing and drowsing, and down he rushes: I 'm in harness again. I can't say it's dead waste of time; besides I pick up an independence for the days ahead. But I don't respect myself for doing the work. Here's the difference between us two servants, Madge: I think of myself, and you don't.'

'The difference is more like between the master and
mistress we serve,
Mr. Gower.'

'Well, I'd rather be the woman in this case.'

'You know the reputation I've got. And can only just read, and can't spell. My mistress teaches me bits of German and French on her walks.'

Gower took a new observation of this girl, whom he had not regarded as like himself, a pushing blade among the grasses. He proposed to continue her lessons, if she cared to learn; saying it could be done in letters.

'I won't be ashamed of writing, if you mean it,' said she. 'My mistress will have a usefuller servant. She had a strange honeymoon of a marriage, if ever was—and told me t' other day she was glad because it brought us together—she a born lady!'

'A fling-above born ladies. She's quick as light to hit on a jewel where there is one, whether it shines or not. She stands among the Verities of the world.'

'Yes,' Madge said, panting for more. 'Do speak of her. When you praise her, I feel she's not wasted. Mistress; and friend and wife—if he'd let her be; and mother; never mother like her. The boy 'll be a sturdy. She'll see he has every chance. He's a lucky little one to have that mother.'

'You think her handsome, Madge?'

Gower asked it, wishing to hear a devotee's confusion of qualities and looks.

The question was a drop on lower spheres, and it required definitions, to touch the exact nature of the form of beauty, and excuse a cooler tone on the commoner plane. These demanded language. She rounded the difficulty, saying: 'You see engravings of archery; that 's her figure— her real figure. I think her face . . . I can't describe . . . it flashes.'

'That's it,' said Gower, delighted with his perception of a bare mind at work and hitting the mark perforce of warmth. 'When it flashes, it's unequalled. There's the supremacy of irregular lines. People talk of perfect beauty: suitable for paintings and statues. Living faces, if they're to show the soul, which is the star on the peak of beauty, must lend themselves to commotion. Nature does it in a breezy tree or over ruffled waters. Repose has never such splendid reach as animation— I mean, in the living face. Artists prefer repose. Only Nature can express the uttermost beauty with her gathering and tuning of discords. Well, your mistress has that beauty. I remember my impression when I saw her first on her mountains abroad. Other beautiful faces of women go pale, grow stale. The diversified in the harmony of the flash are Nature's own, her radiant, made of her many notes, beyond our dreams to reproduce. We can't hope to have a true portrait of your mistress. Does Madge understand?'

The literary dose was a strong one for her; but she saw the index, and got a lift from the sound. Her bosom heaved. 'Oh, I do try, Mr. Gower. I think I do a little. I do more while you're talking. You are good to talk so to me. You should have seen her the night she went to meet my lord at those beastly Gardens Kit Ines told me he was going to. She was defending him. I've no words. You teach me what's meant by poetry. I couldn't understand that once.'

Their eyes were on the countess and her escort in advance. Gower's praises of her mistress's peculiar beauty set the girl compassionately musing. His eloquence upon the beauty was her clue.

Carinthia and Mr. Wythan started at a sharp trot in the direction of the pair of ponies driven by a groom along the curved decline of the narrow roadway. His whip was up for signal.

It concerned the house and the master of it. His groom drove rapidly down, while he hurried on the homeward way, as a man will do, with the dread upon him that his wife's last breath may have been yielded before he can enfold her.

Carinthia walked to be overtaken, not daring to fever her blood at a swifter pace; 'lamed with an infant,' the thought recurred.

'She is very ill, she has fainted, she lies insensible,' Madge heard from her of Mrs. Wythan. 'We were speaking of her when the groom appeared. It has happened twice. They fear the third. He fears it, though he laughs at a superstition. Now step, I know you like walking, Mr. Woodseer. Once I left you behind.'

'I have the whole scene of the angel and the cripple,' Gower replied.

'O that day!'

They 'were soon speculating on the unimpressionable house in its clump of wood midway below, which had no response for anxieties.

A maid-servant at the garden gate, by Mr. Wythan's orders, informed Carinthia that her mistress had opened her eyes: There was a hope of weathering the ominous third time. But the hope was a bird of short flight from bush to bush until the doctor should speak to confirm it. Even the child was under the shadow of the house. Carinthia had him in her arms, trusting to life as she hugged him, and seeing innumerable darts out of all regions assailing her treasure.

'She wishes to have you,' Mr. Wythan came and said to her. 'Almost her first word. The heart is quickening. She will live for me if she can.'

He whispered it. His features shot the sparkle.

Rebecca Wythan had strength to press Carinthia's hand faintly. She made herself heard: 'No pain.' Her husband sat upright, quite still, attentive for any sign. His look of quiet pleasure ready to show, sprightliness dwelt on her. She returned the look, unable to give it greeting. Past the sense of humour, she wanted to say: 'See the poor simple fellow who will think it a wife that he has!' She did but look.

Carinthia spoke his name, 'Mr. Wythan,' by chance, and Rebecca breathed heavily until she formed the words: 'Owain to me.'

'To me,' Owain added.

The three formed a chain of clasped hands.

It was in the mind of the sick lady to disburden herself of more than her weakness could utter, so far was she above earthly links. The desire in her was to be quit of the flesh, bearing a picture of her husband as having the dues of his merits.

Her recovered strength next day brought her nearer to our laws. 'You will call him Owain, Carinthia?' she said. 'He is not one to presume on familiarity. I must be going soon. I cannot leave him the wife I would choose. I can leave him the sister. He is a sure friend. He is the knightly man women dream of. I harp on it because I long for testimony that I leave him to have some reward. And this may be, between two so pure at heart as you two.'

'Dear soul friend, yes, and Owain, yes, I can say it,' Carinthia rejoined. 'Brother? I have only my Chillon. My life is now for him. I am punished for separating myself from the son of my father. I have no heart for a second brother. What I can give to my friend I will. I shall love you in him, if I am to lose you.'

'Not Owain—it was I was the wretch refused to call on the lonely lady at the castle until I heard she had done a romantic little bit of thing— hushed a lambkin's bleating. My loss! my loss! And I could afford it so poorly. Since then Carinthia has filled my days. I shudder to leave you and think of your going back to the English. Their sneer withers. They sent you down among us as a young woman to be shunned.'

'I did wildly, I was ungoverned, I had one idea,' said Carinthia. 'One idea is a bullet, good for the day of battle to beat the foe, father tells us. It was a madness in me. Now it has gone, I see all round. I see straight, too. With one idea, we see nothing—nothing but itself. Whizz! we go. I did. I shall no longer offend in that way. Mr. Gower Woodseer is here from my lord.'

'With him the child will be safe.'

'I am not alarmed. It is to request—they would have me gone, to prepare the way for my lord.'

'You have done, it; he has the castle to himself. I cannot-spare you. A tyrant ordering you to go should be defied. My Lord Fleetwood puts lightning into my slow veins.'

'We have talked: we shall be reproved by the husband and the doctor,' said Carinthia.

Sullen days continued and rolled over to night at the mines. Gower's mission was rendered absurd by the countess's withdrawal from the castle. He spoke of it to Mr. Wythan once, and the latter took a big breath and blew such a lord to the winds. 'Persuade our guest to leave us, that the air may not be tainted for her husband when he comes? He needn't call; he's not obliged to see her. She's offered Esslemont to live in? I believe her instinct's right—he has designs on the child. A little more and we shall have a mad dog in the fellow. He doubles my work by keeping his men out. If she were away we should hear of black doings. Twenty dozen of his pugilists wouldn't stop the burning.'

They agreed that persuasions need not be addressed to the countess. She was and would remain Mr. Wythan's guest. As for the earl, Gower inclined to plead hesitatingly, still to plead, on behalf of a nobleman owning his influence and very susceptible to his wisdom, whose echo of a pointed saying nearly equalled the satisfaction bestowed by print. The titled man affected the philosopher in that manner; or rather, the crude philosopher's relish of brilliant appreciation stripped him of his robe. For he was with Owain Wythan at heart to scorn titles which did not distinguish practical offices. A nation bowing to them has gone to pith, for him; he had to shake himself, that he might not similarly stick; he had to do it often. Objects elevated even by a decayed world have their magnetism for us unless we nerve the mind to wakeful repulsion. He protested he had reason to think the earl was humanizing, though he might be killing a woman in the process. 'Could she wish for better?' he asked, with at least the gravity of the undermining humourist; and he started Owain to course an idea when he remarked of Lord Fleetwood: 'Imagine a devil on his back on a river, flying a cherub.'

Owain sparkled from the vision of the thing to wrath with it.

'Ay, but while he's floating, his people are edging on starvation. And I've a personal grievance. I keep, you know, open hall, bread and cheese and beer, for poor mates. His men are favouring us with a call. We have to cart treble from the town. If I straighten the sticks he dies to bend, it'll be a grievance against me—and a fig for it! But I like to be at peace with my neighbours, and waft them "penillion" instead of dealing the "cleddyfal" of Llewellyn.'

At last the tension ceased; they had intelligence of the earl's arrival.

His countess was little moved by it; and the reason for that lay in her imagination being absorbed. Henrietta had posted her a journal telling of a deed of Chillon's: no great feat, but precious for its 'likeness to him,' as they phrased it; that is, for the light it cast on their conception of the man. Heading a squadron in a riotous Midland town, he stopped a charge, after fire of a shot from the mob, and galloped up the street to catch a staggering urchin to his saddle-bow, and place the mite in safety. Then it was a simple trot of the hussars ahead; way was made for him.

Now, to see what banquet there is for the big of heart in the world's hot stress, take the view of Carinthia, to whom her brother's thoughtful little act of gentleness at the moment of the red-of-the-powder smoke was divinest bread and wine, when calamity hung around, with the future an unfooted wilderness, her powers untried, her husband her enemy.

CHAPTER XXXI
WE HAVE AGAIN TO DEAL WITH THE EXAMPLES OF OUR YOUNGER MAN

The most urgent of Dames is working herself up to a grey squall in her detestation of imagerial epigrams. Otherwise Gower Woodseer's dash at the quintessential young man of wealth would prompt to the carrying of it further, and telling how the tethered flutterer above a 'devil on his back on a river' was beginning to pull if not drag his withholder and teaser.

Fleetwood had almost a desire to see the small dot of humanity which drew the breath from him;—and was indistinguishably the bubbly grin and gurgle of the nurses, he could swear. He kicked at the bondage to our common fleshly nature imposed on him by the mother of the little animal. But there had been a mother to his father: odd movements of a warmish curiosity brushed him when the cynic was not mounting guard. They were, it seemed, external—no part of him: like blasts of a wayside furnace across wintry air. They were, as it chanced, Nature's woman in him plucking at her separated partner, Custom's man; something of an oriental voluptuary on his isolated regal seat; and he would suck the pleasures without a descent into the stale old ruts where Life's convict couple walk linked to one another, to their issue more.

There was also a cold curiosity to see the male infant such a mother would have. The grandson of Old Lawless might turn out a rascal,—he would be no mean one, no coward.

That mother, too, who must have been a touch astonished to find herself a mother:—Fleetwood laughed a curt bark, and heard rebukes, and pleaded the marriage-trap to the man of his word; devil and cherub were at the tug, or say, dog and gentleman, a survival of the schoolboy—that mother, a girl of the mountains, perhaps wanted no more than smoothing by the world. 'It is my husband' sounded foolish, sounded freshish,—a new note. Would she repeat it? The bit of simplicity would bear repeating once. Gower Woodseer says the creature grows and studies to perfect herself. She's a good way off that, and may spoil herself in the process; but she has a certain power. Her donkey obstinacy in refusing compliance, and her pursuit of 'my husband,' and ability to drench him with ridicule, do not exhibit the ordinary young female. She stamps her impression on the people she meets. Her husband is shaken to confess it likewise, despite a disagreement between them.

He has owned he is her husband: he has not disavowed the consequence. That fellow, Gower Woodseer, might accuse the husband of virtually lying, if he by his conduct implied her distastefulness or worse. By heaven! as felon a deed as could be done. Argue the case anyhow, it should be undone. Let her but cease to madden. For whatever the rawness of the woman, she has qualities; and experience of the facile loves of London very sharply defines her qualities. Think of her as raw, she has the gift of rareness: forget the donkey obstinacy, her character grasps. In the grasp of her character, one inclines, and her husband inclines, to become her advocate. She has only to discontinue maddening.

The wealthy young noble prized any form of rareness wherever it was visible, having no thought of the purchase of it, except with worship. He could listen pleased to the talk of a Methodist minister sewing bootleather. He picked up a roadside tramp and made a friend of him, and valued the fellow's honesty, submitted to his lectures, pardoned his insolence. The sight of Carinthia's narrow bedroom and strip of bed over Sarah Winch's Whitechapel shop had gone a step to drown the bobbing Whitechapel Countess. At least, he had not been hunted by that gaunt chalk-quarry ghost since his peep into the room. Own it! she likewise has things to forgive. Women nurse their larvae of ideas about fair dealing. But observe the distinction: aid if women understood justice they would be the first to proclaim, that when two are tied together, the one who does the other serious injury is more naturally excused than the one who-tenfold abhorrent if a woman!—calls up the grotesque to extinguish both.

With this apology for himself, Lord Fleetwood grew tolerant of the person honourably avowed as his wife. So; therefore, the barrier between him and his thoughts of her was broken. The thoughts carrying red doses were selected. Finally, the taste to meet her sprouted. If agreeable, she could be wooed; if barely agreeable, tormented; if disagreeable, left as before.

Although it was the hazard of a die, he decided to follow his taste. Her stay at the castle had kept him long from the duties of his business; and he could imagine it a grievance if he pleased, but he put it aside. Alighting at his chief manager's office, he passed through the heated atmosphere of black-browed, wiry little rebels, who withheld the salute as they lounged: a posture often preceding the spring in compulsorily idle workers. He was aware of instinct abroad, an antagonism to the proprietor's rights. They roused him to stand by them, and were his own form of instinct, handsomely clothed. It behoved that he should examine them and the claims against them, to be sure of his ground. He and Mr. Howell Edwards debated the dispute for an hour; agreeing, partially differing. There was a weakness on the principle in Edwards. These fellows fixed to the spot are for compromise too much. An owner of mines has no steady reckoning of income if the rate of wage is perpetually to shift according to current, mostly ignorant, versions of the prosperity of the times. Are we so prosperous? It is far from certain. And if the rate ascends, the question of easing it down to suit the discontinuance of prosperity agitating our exchequer—whose demand is for fixity— perplexes us further.

However, that was preliminary. He and Howell Edwards would dine and wrangle it out. The earl knew himself a hot disputant after dinner. Incidentally he heard of Lady Fleetwood as a guest of Mrs. Wythan; and the circumstance was injurious to him because he stood against Mr. Wythan's pampering system with his men.

Ines up at the castle smelt of beer, and his eyelids were sottish. Nothing to do tries the virtue of the best. He sought his excuse in a heavy lamentation over my lady's unjust suspicion of him,—a known man of honour, though he did serve his paytron.

The cause of Lady Fleetwood's absence was exposed to her outraged lord, who had sent the man purely to protect her at this castle, where she insisted on staying. The suspicion cast on the dreary lusher was the wife's wild shot at her husband. One could understand a silly woman's passing terror. Her acting under the dictate of it struck the husband's ribbed breast as a positive clap of hostilities between them across a chasm.

His previous placable mood was immediately conceived by him to have been one of his fits of generosity; a step to a frightful dutiful embrace of an almost repulsive object. He flung the thought of her back on her Whitechapel. She returned from that place with smiles, dressed in a laundry white with a sprinkle of smuts, appearing to him as an adversary armed and able to strike. There was a blow, for he chewed resentments; and these were goaded by a remembered shyness of meeting her eyes when he rounded up the slope of the hill, in view of his castle, where he supposed she would be awaiting 'my husband.' The silence of her absence was lively mockery of that anticipation.

Gower came on him sauntering about the grounds.

'You're not very successful down here,' Fleetwood said, without greeting.

'The countess likes the air of this country,' said Gower, evasively, impertinently, and pointlessly; offensively to the despot employing him to be either subservient or smart.

'I wish her to leave it.'

'She wishes to see you first.'

'She takes queer measures. I start to-morrow for my yacht at Cardiff.' There the matter ended; for Fleetwood fell to talking of the mines. At dinner and after dinner it was the topic, and after Howell Edwards had departed.

When the man who has a heart will talk of nothing but what concerns his interests, and the heart is hurt, it may be perceived by a cognizant friend, that this is his proud mute way of petitioning to have the tenderer subject broached. Gower was sure of the heart, armoured or bandaged though it was,—a haunt of evil spirits as well,—and he began: 'Now to speak of me half a minute. You cajoled me out of my Surrey room, where I was writing, in the vein . . .'

'I've had the scene before me!' the earl interposed. 'Juniper dells and that tree of the flashing leaf, and that dear old boy, your father, young as you and me, and saying love of Nature gives us eternal youth. On with you.'

'I doubted whether I should be of use to you. I told you the amount of alloy in my motives. A year with you, I have subsistence for ten years assured to me.'

'Don't be a prosy dog, Gower Woodseer.'

'Will you come over to the Wythans before you go?'

'I will not.'

'You would lengthen your stride across a wounded beast?'

'I see no wound to the beast.'

'You can permit yourself to kick under cover of a metaphor.'

'Tell me what you drive at, Gower.'

'The request is, for you to spare pain by taking one step—an extra strain on the muscles of the leg. It 's only the leg wants moving.'

'The lady has legs to run away, let them bring her back.'

'Why have me with you, then? I'm useless. But you read us all, see everything, and wait only for the mood to do the right. You read me, and I'm not open to everybody. You read the crux of a man like me in my novel position. You read my admiration of a beautiful woman and effort to keep honest. You read my downright preference of what most people would call poverty, and my enjoyment of good cookery and good company. You enlist among the crew below as one of our tempters. You find I come round to the thing I like best. Therefore, you have your liking for me; and that's why you turn to me again, after your natural infidelities. So much for me. You read this priceless lady quite as clearly. You choose to cloud her with your moods. She was at a disadvantage, 'arriving in a strange country, next to friendless; and each new incident bred of a luckless beginning—I could say more.'

Fleetwood nodded. 'You are read without the words: You read in history, too, I suppose, that there are two sides to most cases. The loudest is not often the strongest. However, now the lady shows herself crazed. That's reading her charitably. Else she has to be taken for a spiteful shrew, who pretends to suspect anything that's villanous, because she can hit on no other way of striking.'

'Crazed, is a wide shot and hits half the world,' muttered Gower. 'Lady Fleetwood had a troubled period after her marriage. She suffered a sort of kidnapping when she was bearing her child. There's a book by an Edinburgh doctor might be serviceable to you. It enlightens me. She will have a distrust of you, as regards the child, until she understands you by living with you under one roof.'

'Such animals these women are!' Good Lord !'

Fleetwood ejaculated.

'I marry one, and I 'm to take to reading medical books!'

He yawned.

'You speak that of women and pretend to love Nature,' said Gower. 'You hate Nature unless you have it served on a dish by your own cook. That's the way to the madhouse or the monastery. There we expiate the sin of sins. A man finds the woman of all women fitted to stick him in the soil, and trim and point him to grow, and she's an animal for her pains! The secret of your malady is, you've not yet, though you're on a healthy leap for the practices of Nature, hopped to the primary conception of what Nature means. Women are in and of Nature. I've studied them here—had nothing to do but study them. That most noble of ladies' whole mind was knotted to preserve her child during her time of endurance up to her moment of trial. Think it over. It's your one chance of keeping sane.

And expect to hear flat stuff from me while you go on playing tyrant.'

'You certainly take liberties,' Fleetwood's mildest voice remarked.

'I told you I should try you, when you plucked me out of my Surrey nest.'

Fleetwood, passed from a meditative look to a malicious half-laugh. 'You seem to have studied the "most noble of ladies" latterly rather like a barrister with a brief for the defendant—plaintiff, if you like!'

'As to that, I'll help you to an insight of a particular weakness of mine,' said Gower. 'I require to have persons of even the highest value presented to me on a stage, or else I don't grasp them at all—they 're simply pictures. I saw the lady; admired, esteemed, sufficiently, I supposed, until her image appeared to me in the feelings of another. Then I saw fathoms. No doubt, it was from feeling warmer. I went through the blood of the other for my impression.'

'Name the other,' said the earl, and his features were sharp.

You can have the name,' Gower answered. 'It was the girl, Madge Winch.'

Fleetwood's hard stare melted to surprise and contemptuous amusement. 'You see the lady to be the "most noble of ladies" through the warming you get by passing into the feelings of Madge Winch?'

Sarcasm was in the tone, and beneath it a thrill of compassionateness traversed him and shot a remorseful sting with the vision of those two young women on the coach at the scene of the fight. He had sentience of their voices, nigh to hearing them. The forlorn bride's hand given to the anxious girl behind her gushed an image of the sisterhood binding women under the pangs they suffer from men. He craved a scourging that he might not be cursing himself; and he provoked it, for Gower was very sensitive to a cold breath on the weakness he had laid bare; and when Fleetwood said: 'You recommend a bath in the feelings of Madge Winch?' the retort came:—'It might stop you on the road to a cowl.'

Fleetwood put on the mask of cogitation to cover a shudder, 'How?'

'A question of the man or the monk with you, as I fancy I've told you more than once!'

'You may fancy committing any impertinence and be not much out.'

'The saving of you is that you digest it when you've stewed it down.'

'You try me!'

'I don't impose the connection.'

'No, I take the blame for that.'

They sat in dumbness, fidgeted, sprang to their feet, and lighted bedroom candles.

Mounting the stairs, Gower was moved to let fall a benevolent look on the worried son of fortune. 'I warned you I should try you. It ought to be done politely. If I have to speak a truth I 'm boorish. The divinely damnable naked truth won't wear ornaments. It's about the same as pitching a handful of earth.'

'You dirt your hands, hit or miss. Out of this corridor! Into my room, and spout your worst,' cried the earl.

Gower entered his dressing-room and was bidden to smoke there.

'You're a milder boor when you smoke. That day down in Surrey with the grand old bootmaker was one of our days, Gower Woodseer! There's no smell of the boor in him. Perhaps his religion helps him, more than Nature-worship: not the best for manners. You won't smoke your pipe? —a cigar? Lay on, then, as hard as you like.'

'You're asking for the debauchee's last luxury—not a correction,' said Gower, grimly thinking of how his whip might prove effective and punish the man who kept him fruitlessly out of his bed.

'I want stuff for a place in the memory,' said Fleetwood; and the late hour, with the profitless talk, made it a stinging taunt.

'You want me to flick your indecision.'

'That's half a hit.'

'I 'm to talk italics, for you to store a smart word or so.'

'True, I swear! And, please, begin.'

'You hang for the Fates to settle which is to be smothered in you, the man or the lord—and it ends in the monk, if you hang much longer.'

'A bit of a scorpion in his intention,' Fleetwood
muttered on a stride.
'I'll tell you this, Gower Woodseer; when you lay on in
earnest, your diction is not so choice. Do any of your
remarks apply to Lady Fleetwood?'

'All should. I don't presume to allude to Lady Fleetwood.'

'She has not charged you to complain?'

' Lady Fleetwood is not the person to complain or condescend to speak of injuries.'

'She insults me with her insane suspicion.'

A swollen vein on the young nobleman's forehead went to confirm the idea at the Wythans' that he was capable of mischief. They were right; he was as capable of villany as of nobility. But he happened to be thanking Gower Woodseer's whip for the comfortable numbness he felt at Carinthia's behaviour, while detesting her for causing him to desire it and endure it, and exonerate his prosy castigator.

He was ignorant of the revenge he had on Gower, whose diction had not been particularly estimable. In the feebleness of a man vainly courting sleep, the disarmed philosopher tossed from one side to the other through the remaining hours of darkness, polishing sentences that were natural spouts of choicest diction; and still the earl's virulent small sneer rankled. He understood why, after a time. The fervour of advocacy, which inspires high diction, had been wanting. He had sought more to lash the earl with his personal disgust and partly to parade his contempt of a lucrative dependency—than he had felt for the countess. No wonder his diction was poor. It was a sample of limp thinness; a sort of tongue of a Master Slender:—flavourless, unsatisfactory, considering its object: measured to be condemned by its poor achievement. He had nevertheless a heart to feel for the dear lady, and heat the pleading for her, especially when it ran to its object, as along a shaft of the sun- rays, from the passionate devotedness of that girl Madge.

He brooded over it till it was like a fire beneath him to drive him from his bed and across the turfy roller of the hill to the Wythans', in the front of an autumnal sunrise—grand where the country is shorn of surface decoration, as here and there we find some unadorned human creature, whose bosom bears the ball of warmth.

CHAPTER XXXII IN WHICH WE SEE CARINTHIA PUT IN PRACTICE ONE OF HER OLD FATHER'S LESSONS

Seated at his breakfast-table, the earl saw Gower stride in, and could have wagered he knew the destination of the fellow's morning walk. It concerned him little; he would be leaving the castle in less than an hour. She might choose to come or choose to keep away. The whims of animals do not affect men unless they are professionally tamers. Petty domestic dissensions are besides poor webs to the man pulling singlehanded at ropes with his revolted miners. On the topic of wages, too, he was Gower's master, and could hold forth: by which he taught himself to feel that practical affairs are the proper business of men, women and infants being remotely secondary; the picturesque and poetry, consequently, sheer nonsense.

'I suppose your waiting here is useless, to quote you,' he said. 'The countess can decide now to remain, if she pleases. Drive with me to Cardiff—I miss you if you 're absent a week. Or is it legs? Drop me a line of your stages on the road, and don't loiter much.'

Gower spoke of starting his legs next day, if he had to do the journey alone: and he clouded the yacht for Fleetwood with talk of the Wye and the Usk, Hereford and the Malvern Hills elliptical over the plains

'Yes,' the earl acquiesced jealously; 'we ought to have seen—tramped every foot of our own country. That yacht of mine, there she is, and I said I would board her and have a fly with half a dozen fellows round the Scottish isles. We're never free to do as we like.'

'Legs are the only things that have a taste of freedom,' said Gower.

They strolled down to Howell Edwards' office at nine, Kit Ines beside the luggage cart to the rear.

Around the office and along to the street of the cottages crowds were chattering, gesticulating; Ines fancied the foreign jabberers inclined to threaten. Howell Edwards at the door of his office watched them calculatingly. The lord of their destinies passed in with him, leaving Gower to study the features of the men, and Ines to reckon the chance of a fray.

Fleetwood came out presently, saying to Edwards:

'That concession goes far enough. Because I have a neighbour who yields at every step? No, stick to the principle. I've said my final word. And here's the carriage. If the mines are closed, more's the pity: but I'm not responsible. You can let them know if you like, before I drive off; it doesn't matter to me.'

The carriage was ready. Gower cast a glance up the hill. Three female figures and a pannier-donkey were visible on the descent. He nodded to Edwards, who took the words out of his mouth. 'Her ladyship, my lord.'

She was distinctly seen, and looked formidable in definition against the cloud. Madge and the nurse-maid Martha were the two other young women. On they came, and the, angry man seated in the carriage could not give the order to start. Nor could he quite shape an idea of annoyance, though he hung to it and faced at Gower a battery of the promise to pay him for this. Tattling observers were estimated at their small importance there, as everywhere, by one so high above them. But the appearance of the woman of the burlesque name and burlesque actions, and odd ascension out of the ludicrous into a form to cast a spell, so that she commanded serious recollections of her, disturbed him. He stepped from his carriage. Again he had his incomprehensible fit of shyness; and a vision of the complacent, jowled, redundant, blue-coated monarch aswing in imbecile merriment on the signboard of the Royal Sovereign inn; constitutionally his total opposite, yet instigating the sensation.

In that respect his countess and he had shifted characters. Carinthia came on at her bold mountain stride to within hail of him. Met by Gower, she talked, smiled, patted her donkey, clutched his ear, lifted a silken covering to show the child asleep; entirely at her ease and unhurried. These women get aid from their pride of maternity. And when they can boast a parson behind them, they are indecorous up to insolent in their ostentation of it.

She resumed her advance, with a slight abatement of her challengeing match, sedately; very collectedly erect; changed in the fulness of her figure and her poised calm bearing.

He heard her voice addressing Gower: 'Yes, they do; we noticed the slate- roofs, looking down on them. They do look like a council of rooks in the hollow; a parliament, you said. They look exceedingly like, when a peep of sunshine falls. Oh, no; not clergymen!'

She laughed at the suggestion.

She might be one of the actresses by nature.

Is the man unsympathetic with women a hater of Nature deductively? Most women are actresses. As to worshipping Nature, we go back to the state of heathen beast, Mr. Philosopher Gower could be answered . . . .

Fleetwood drew in his argument. She stood before him. There was on his part an insular representation of old French court salute to the lady, and she replied to it in the exactest measure, as if an instructed proficient.

She stood unshadowed. 'We have come to bid you adieu, my lord,' she said, and no trouble of the bosom shook her mellow tones. Her face was not the chalk-quarry or the rosed rock; it was oddly individual, and, in a way, alluring, with some gentle contraction of her eyelids. But evidently she stood in full repose, mistress of herself.

Upon him, it appeared, the whole sensibility of the situation was to be thrown. He hardened.

'We have had to settle business here,' he said, speaking resonantly, to cover his gazing discomposedly, all but furtively.

The child was shown, still asleep. A cunning infant not a cry in him to excuse a father for preferring concord or silence or the bachelor's exemption.

'He is a strong boy,' the mother said. 'Our doctor promises he will ride over all the illnesses.'

Fleetwood's answer set off with an alarum of the throat,
and dwindled to 'We 'll hope so. Seems to sleep well.'

She had her rocky brows. They were not barren crags, and her shape was Nature's ripeness, it was acknowledged: She stood like a lance in air-rather like an Amazon schooled by Athene, one might imagine. Hues of some going or coming flush hinted the magical trick of her visage. She spoke in modest manner, or it might be indifferently, without a flaunting of either.

'I wish to consult you, my lord. He is not baptized. His Christian names?'

'I have no choice.'

'I should wish him to bear one of my brother's names.'

'I have no knowledge of your brother's names.'

'Chillon is one.'

'Ah! Is it, should you think, suitable to our climate?'

'Another name of my brother's is John.'

'Bull.' The loutish derision passed her and rebounded on him. 'That would be quite at home.'

'You will allow one of your own names, my lord?'

'Oh, certainly, if you desire it, choose. There are four names you will find in a book of the Peerage or Directory or so. Up at the castle—or you might have written:—better than these questions on the public road. I don't demur. Let it be as you like.'

'I write empty letters to tell what I much want,' Carinthia said.

'You have only to write your plain request.'

'If, now I see you, I may speak another request, my lord.'

'Pray,' he said, with courteous patience, and stepped forward down to the street of the miners' cottages. She could there speak out-bawl the request, if it suited her to do so.

On the point of speaking, she gazed round.

'Perfectly safe! no harm possible,' said he, fretful under the burden of this her maniacal maternal anxiety.

'The men are all right, they would not hurt a child. What can rationally be suspected!'

'I know the men; they love their children,' she replied. 'I think my child would be precious to them. Mr. Woodseer and Mr. Edwards and Madge are there.'

'Is the one more request—I mean, a mother's anxiety does not run to the extent of suspecting everybody?'

'Some of the children are very pretty,' said Carinthia, and eyed the bands of them at their games in the roadway and at the cottage doors. 'Children of the poor have happy mothers.'

Her eyes were homely, morning over her face. They were open now to what that fellow Woodseer (who could speak to the point when he was not aiming at it) called the parlour, or social sitting-room; where we may have converse with the tame woman's mind, seeing the door to the clawing recesses temporarily shut.

'Forgive me if I say you talk like the bigger child,' Fleetwood said lightly, not ungenially; for the features he looked on were museful, a picture in their one expression.

Her answer chilled him. 'It is true, my lord. I will not
detain you.
I would beg to be supplied with money.'

He was like the leaves of a frosted plant, in his crisp curling inward:—he had been so genial.

'You have come to say good-bye, that an opportunity to—as you put it— beg for money. I am not sure of your having learnt yet the right disposal of money.'

'I beg, my lord, to have two thousand pounds a year allowed me.'

'Ten—and it's a task to spend the sum on a single
household—shall be alloted to your expenditure at
Esslemont;—stables, bills, et caetera.
You can entertain. My steward Leddings will undertake
the management.
You will not be troubled with payings.'

Her head acknowledged the graciousness.—'I would have two thousand pounds and live where I please.'

'Pardon me: the two, for a lady living where she pleases, exceeds the required amount.'

'I will accept a smaller sum, my lord.'

'Money!-it seems a singular demand when all supplies are furnished.'

'I would have control of some money.'

'You are thinking of charities.'

'Not charities.'

'Edwards here has a provision for the hospital needs of the people. Mr. Woodseer applies to me in cases he can certify. Leddings will do the same at Esslemont.'

'I am glad, I am thankful. The money I would have is for
my own use.
It is for me.'

'Ah. Scarcely that, I fancy.'

The remark should have struck home. He had a thirst for the sign of her confessing to it. He looked. Something like a petrifaction of her wildest face was shown.

Carinthia's eyes were hard out on a scattered knot of children down the street.

She gathered up her skirts. Without a word to him, she
ran, and running shouted to the little ones around and
ahead: 'In! in! indoors, children!
"Blant, i'r ty!" Mothers, mothers, ho! get them in. See the

dog! "Ci!
Ci!" In with them! "Blant, i'r ty! Vr ty!"'

A big black mongrel appeared worrying at one of two petticoated urchins on the ground.

She scurried her swiftest, with such warning Welsh as she had on the top of her mountain cry; and doors flew wide, there was a bang of doors when she darted by: first gust of terrible heavens that she seemed to the cottagers.

Other shouts behind her rent the air, gathering to a roar, from the breasts of men and women. 'Mad dog about' had been for days the rumour, crossing the hills over the line of village, hamlet, farm, from Cardiff port.

Dead hush succeeded the burst. Men and women stood off. The brute was at the lady.

Her arms were straight above her head; her figure overhanging, on a bend of the knees. Right and left, the fury of the slavering fangs shook her loose droop of gown; and a dull, prolonged growl, like the clamour of a far body of insurrectionary marching men, told of the rage.

Fleetwood hovered helpless as a leaf on a bough.

'Back—', I pray,' she said to him, and motioned it, her arms at high stretch.

He held no weapon. The sweat of his forehead half blinded him. And she waved him behind her, beckoned to the crowd to keep wide way, used her lifted hands as flappers; she had all her wits. There was not a wrinkle of a grimace. Nothing but her locked lips betrayed her vision of imminent doom. The shaking of her gown and the snarl in the undergrowl sounded insatiate.

The brute dropped hold. With a weariful jog of the head, it pursued its course at an awful even swinging pace: Death's own, Death's doer, his reaper,—he, the very Death of the Terrors.

Carinthia's cry rang for clear way to be kept on either side, and that accursed went the path through a sharp-edged mob, as it poured pell-mell and shrank back, closing for the chase to rear of it.

'Father taught me,' she said to the earl, not more discomposed than if she had taken a jump.

'It's over!' he groaned, savagely white, and bellowed for guns, any weapons. 'Your father? pray?' She was entreated to speak.

'Yes, it must be shot; it will be merciful to kill it,' she said. 'They have carried the child indoors. The others are safe. Mr. Woodseer, run to my nurse-girl, Martha. He goes,' she murmured, and resumed to the earl: 'Father told me women have a better chance than men with a biting dog. He put me before him and drilled me. He thought of everything. Usually the poor beast snaps—one angry bite, not more. My dress teased it.'

Fleetwood grinned civilly in his excitement; intending to yield patient hearing, to be interested by any mortal thing she might choose to say.

She was advised by recollection to let her father rest.

'No, dear girl, not hurt, no scratch,—only my gown torn,' she said to Madge; and Madge heaved and whimpered, and stooped to pin the frayed strips. 'Quite safe; you see it is easy for women to escape, Mr. Edwards.'

Carinthia's voice hummed over the girl's head

'Father made me practise it, in case. He forethought. Madge, you heard of this dog. I told you how to act. I was not feverish. Our babe will not feel it.'

She bade Madge open her hands. 'A scratch would kill.
Never mind the tearings; I will hold my dress. Oh! there is that one child bitten.
Mr. Edwards, mount a man for the doctor. I will go in to the child.
He was bitten. Lose not one minute, Mr. Edwards. I see you go.'

He bowed and hastened.

The child's mother was red eyes at her door for ease of her heart to the lady. Carinthia stepped into the room, where the little creature was fetching sobs after the spout of screams.

'God in heaven! she can't be going to suck the bite?' Fleetwood cried to Madge, whose answer was disquieting 'If it's to save life, my mistress won't stop at anything.'

His heart sprang with a lighted comprehension of Gower Woodseer's meaning. This girl's fervour opened portals to new views of her mistress, or opened eyes.

CHAPTER XXXIII
A FRIGHTFUL DEBATE

Pushing through a swarm into the cot, Fleetwood saw Carinthia on a knee beside a girl's lap, where the stripped child lay. Its mother held a basin for the dabbing at raw red spots.

A sting of pain touched the memory of its fright, and brought further screams, then the sobs. Carinthia hummed a Styrian cradle-song as the wailing lulled.

She glanced up; she said to the earl: 'The bite was deep; it was in the blood. We may have time. Get me an interpreter. I must ask the mother. I know not many words.'

'What now?' said he, at the looming of new vexations.

'We have no choice. Has a man gone? Dr. Griffiths would hurry fast. An hour may be too late. The poison travels: Father advised it:—Fifty years for one brave minute! This child should be helped to live.'

'We 'll do our best. Why an interpreter?'

'A poker in the fire. The interpreter—whether the mother will bear to have it done.'

'Burn, do you mean?'

'It should be burnt.'

'Not by you?'

'Quick! Quick!'

'But will you—could you? No, I say!'

'If there is no one else.'

'You forget your own child.'

'He is near the end of his mother.'

'The doctor will soon arrive.'

'The poison travels. It cannot be overtaken unless we start nearly equal, father said.'

'Work like that wants an experienced hand.'

'A steady one. I would not quake—not tremble.'

'I cannot permit it.'

'Mr. Wythan would know!—he would know!

'Do you hear, Lady Fleetwood—the dog may not be mad!'

'Signs! He ran heavy, he foamed.'

'Foam 's no sign.'

'Go; order to me a speaker of English and Welsh.'

The earl spun round, sensible of the novelty of his being commanded, and submitting; but no sooner had he turned than he fell into her view of the urgency, and he went, much like the boy we see at school, with a strong hand on his collar running him in.

Madge entered, and said: 'Mr. Woodseer has seen baby and Martha and the donkey all safe.'

'He is kind,' said Carinthia. 'Do we right to bathe the wound? It seems right to wash it. Little things that seem right may be exactly wrong after all, when we are ignorant. I know burning the wound is right.'

Madge asked: 'But, my lady, who is to do it?'

'You would do it, dear, if I shrank,' her mistress replied.

'Oh, my lady, I don't know, I can't say. Burning a child! And there's our baby.'

'He has had me nearly his time.'

'Oh, my dear lady! Would the mother consent?'

'My Madge! I have so few of their words yet. You would hold the child to save it from a dreadful end.'

'God help me, my lady—I would, as long as I live I will . . . . Oh! poor infant, we do need our courage now.'

Seeing that her mistress had not a tear or a tremor, the girl blinked and schooled her quailing heart, still under the wicked hope that the mother would not consent; in a wonderment at this lady, who was womanly, and who could hold the red iron at living flesh, to save the poor infant from a dreadful end. Her flow of love to this dear lady felt the slicing of a cut; was half revulsion, half worship; uttermost worship in estrangement, with the further throbbing of her pulses.

The cottage door was pushed open for Lord Fleetwood and Howell Edwards, whom his master had prepared to stand against immediate operations. A mounted messenger had been despatched. But it was true, the doctor might not be at home. Assuming it to be a bite of rabies, minutes lost meant the terrible: Edwards bowed his head to that. On the other hand, he foresaw the closest of personal reasons for hesitating to be in agreement with the lady wholly. The countess was not so much a persuasive lady as she was, in her breath and gaze, a sweeping and a wafting power. After a short argument, he had the sense of hanging like a bank detached to fatality of motion by the crack of a landslip, and that he would speedily be on his manhood to volunteer for the terrible work.

He addressed the mother. Her eyes whitened from their red at his first word of laying hot iron on the child: she ran out with the wild woman's howl to her neighbours.

> 'Poor mother!' Carinthia sighed. 'It may last a year in
> the child's body, and one day he shudders at water.
> Father saw a bitten man die.
> I could fear death with the thought of that poison in me.
> I pray Dr. Griffiths may come.'

Fleetwood shuffled a step. 'He will come, he will come.'

The mother and some women now packed the room.

A gabble arose between them and Edwards. They fired sharp snatches of speech, and they darted looks at the lady and her lord.

'They do not know!' said Carinthia.

Gower brought her news that the dog had been killed; Martha and her precious burden were outside, a mob of men, too. He was not alarmed; but she went to the door and took her babe in her arms, and when the women observed the lady holding her own little one, their looks were softened. At a hint of explanation from Edwards, the guttural gabble rattled up to the shrill vowels.

Fleetwood's endurance broke short. The packed small room, the caged-monkey lingo, the wailful child, and the past and apprehended debate upon the burning of flesh, composed an intolerable torture. He said to Edwards: 'Go to the men; settle it with them. We have to follow that man Wythan; no peace otherwise. Tell the men the body of the dog must be secured for analysis. Mad or not, it's the same. These Welsh mothers and grandmothers won't allow cautery at any price. Hark at them!'

He turned to Carinthia: 'Your ladyship will let Mr. Edwards or Mr. Woodseer conduct you to the house where you are residing. You don't know these excitable people. I wish you to leave.'

She replied softly: 'I stay for the doctor's coming.'

'Impossible for me to wait, and I can't permit you to be here.'

'It is life and death, and I must not be commanded.'

'You may be proposing gratuitous agony.'

'I would do it to my own child.'

The earl attacked Gower: 'Add your voice to persuade Lady Fleetwood.'

Gower said: 'What if I think with Lady Fleetwood?'

'You would see her do it?'

'Do it myself, if there was no one else'

'This dog-all of you have gone mad,' the earl cried.

'Griffiths may keep his head; it's the only chance. Take my word, these Welshwomen just listen to them won't have it. You 'll find yourself in a nest of Furies. It may be right to do, it's folly to propose it, madness to attempt it. And I shall be bitten if I stop here a minute longer; I'm gone; I can neither command nor influence. I should have thought Gower Woodseer would have kept his wits.'

Fleetwood's look fell on Madge amid the group. Gower's perception of her mistress through the girl's devotion to her moved him. He took Madge by the hand, and the sensation came that it was the next thing to pressing his wife's. 'You're a loyal girl. You have a mistress it 's an honour to serve. You bind me. By the way, Ines shall run down for a minute before I go.'

'Let him stay where he is,'' Madge said, having bobbed her curtsey.

'Oh, if he's not to get a welcome!' said the earl; and he could now fix a steadier look on his countess, who would have animated him with either a hostile face or a tender. She had no expression of a feeling. He bent to her formally.

Carinthia's words were: 'Adieu, my lord.'

'I have only to say, that Esslemont is ready to receive you,' he remarked, bowed more curtly, and walked out. . .

Gower followed him. They might as well have been silent, for any effect from what was uttered between them. They spoke opinions held by each of them—adverse mainly; speaking for no other purpose than to hold their positions.

'Oh, she has courage, no doubt; no one doubted it,' Fleetwood said, out of all relation to the foregoing.

Courage to grapple with his pride and open his heart was wanting in him.

Had that been done, even to the hint of it, instead of the lordly indifference shown, Gower might have ventured on a suggestion, that the priceless woman he could call wife was fast slipping away from him and withering in her allegiance. He did allude to his personal sentiment. 'One takes aim at Philosophy; Lady Fleetwood pulls us up to pay tribute to our debts.' But this was vague, and his hearer needed a present thunder and lightning to shake and pierce him.

'I pledged myself to that yacht,' said Fleetwood, by way of reply, 'or you and I would tramp it, as we did once-jolly old days! I shall have you in mind. Now turn back. Do the best you can.'

They parted midway up the street, Gower bearing away a sharp contrast of the earl and his countess; for, until their senses are dulled, impressionable young men, however precociously philosophical, are mastered by appearances; and they have to reflect under new lights before vision of the linked eye and mind is given them.

Fleetwood jumped into his carriage and ordered the coachman to drive smartly. He could not have admitted the feeling small; he felt the having been diminished, and his requiring a rapid transportation from these parts for him to regain his proper stature. Had he misconducted himself at the moment of danger? It is a ghastly thought, that the craven impulse may overcome us. But no, he could reassure his repute for manliness. He had done as much as a man could do in such a situation.

At the same time, he had done less than the woman.

Needed she to have gone so far? Why precipitate herself into the jaws of the beast?

Now she, proposes to burn the child's wound. And she will do it if they let her. One, sees her at the work,—pale, flinty; no faces; trebly the terrific woman in her mild way of doing the work. All because her old father recommended it. Because she thinks it a duty, we will say; that is juster. This young woman is a very sword in the hand of her idea of duty. She can be feminine, too,—there is one who knows. She can be particularly distant, too. If in timidity, she has a modest view of herself—or an enormous conception of the magi that married her. Will she take the world's polish a little?

Fleetwood asked with the simplicity of the superior being who will consequently perhaps bestow the debt he owes. . .

But his was not the surface nature which can put a question of the sort and pass it. As soon as it had been formed, a vision of the elemental creature calling him husband smote to shivers the shell we walk on, and caught him down among the lower forces, up amid the higher; an infernal and a celestial contest for the extinction of the one or the other of them, if it was not for their union. She wrestled with him where the darknesses roll their snake-eyed torrents over between jagged horns of the netherworld. She stood him in the white ray of the primal vital heat, to bear unwithering beside her the test of light. They flew, they chased, battled, embraced, disjoined, adventured apart, brought back the count of their deeds, compared them,—and name the one crushed! It was the one weighted to shame, thrust into the cellar-corner of his own disgust, by his having asked whether that starry warrior spirit in the woman's frame would 'take polish a little.'

Why should it be a contention between them? For this reason: he was reduced to admire her act; and if he admired, he could not admire without respecting; if he respected, perforce he reverenced; if he reverenced, he worshipped. Therefore she had him at her feet. At the feet of any woman, except for the trifling object! But at the feet of 'It is my husband!' That would be a reversal of things.

Are not things reversed when the name Carinthia sounds in the thought of him who laughed at the name not less angelically martial than Feltre's adored silver trumpets of his Papal procession; sweeter of the new morning for the husband of the woman; if he will but consent to the worshipper's posture? Yes, and when Gower Woodseer's 'Malady of the Wealthy,' as he terms the pivotting of the whole marching and wheeling world upon the favoured of Fortune's habits and tastes, promises to quit its fell clutch on him?

Another voice in the young nobleman cried: Pooh, dolt and dupe! and surrounded her for half a league with reek of burnt flesh and shrieks of a tortured child; giving her the aspect of a sister of the Parcw. But it was not the ascendant' voice. It growled underneath, much like the deadly beast at Carinthia's gown while she stood:—an image of her to dominate the princeliest of men.

The princeliest must have won his title to the place before he can yield other than complimentary station to a woman without violation of his dignity; and vast wealth is not the title; worldly honours are not; deeds only are the title. Fleetwood consented to tell himself that he had not yet performed the deeds.

Therefore, for him to be dominated was to be obscured, eclipsed. A man may outrun us; it is the fortune of war. Eclipsed behind the skirts of a woman waving her upraised hands, with, 'Back, pray!'—no, that ignominy is too horribly abominable! Be sure, the situation will certainly recur in some form; will constantly recur. She will usurp the lead; she will play the man.

Let matters go on as they are. We know our personal worth.

Arrived at this point in the perpetual round of the conflict Carinthia had implanted, Fleetwood entered anew the ranks of the ordinary men of wealth and a coronet, and he hugged himself. He enjoyed repose; knowing it might be but a truce. Matters might go on as they were. Still, he wished her away from those Wythans, residing at Esslemont. There she might come eventually to a better knowledge of his personal worth:—'the gold mine we carry in our bosoms till it is threshed out of us in sweat,' that fellow Gower Woodseex says; adding, that we are the richer for not exploring it. Philosophical cynicism is inconclusive. Fleetwood knew his large capacities; he had proved them and could again. In case a certain half foreseen calamity should happen:—imagine it a fact, imagine him seized, besides admiring her character, with a taste for her person! Why, then, he would have to impress his own mysteriously deep character on her portion of understanding. The battle for domination would then begin.

Anticipation of the possibility of it hewed division between the young man's pride of being and his warmer feelings. Had he been free of the dread of subjection, he would have sunk to kiss the feet of the statuesque young woman, arms in air, firm-fronted over the hideous death that tore at her skirts.

CHAPTER XXXIV
A SURVEY OF THE RIDE OF THE WELSH CAVALIERS ESCORTING THE COUNTESS OF FLEETWOOD TO KENTISH ESSLEMONT

A formal notification from the earl, addressed to the Countess of Fleetwood in the third person, that Esslemont stood ready to receive her, autocratically concealed her lord's impatience to have her there; and by the careful precision with which the stages of her journey were marked, as places where the servants despatched to convey their lady would find preparations for her comfort, again alarmed the disordered mother's mind on behalf of the child she deemed an object of the father's hatred, second to his hatred of the mother. But the mother could defend herself, the child was prey. the child of a detested wife was heir to his title and estates. His look at the child, his hasty one look down at her innocent, was conjured before her as resembling a kick at a stone in his path. His indifference to the child's Christian names pointed darkly over its future.

The distempered wilfulness of a bruised young woman directed her thoughts. She spoke them in the tone of reason to her invalid friend Rebecca Wythan, who saw with her, felt with her, yearned to retain her till breath was gone. Owain Wythan had his doubts of the tyrant guilty of maltreating this woman of women. 'But when you do leave Wales,' he said, 'you shall be guarded up to your haven.'

Carinthia was not awake to his meaning then. She sent a short letter of reply, imitating the style of her lord; very baldly stating, that she was unable to leave Wales because of her friend's illness and her part as nurse. Regrets were unmentioned.

Meanwhile Rebecca Wythan was passing to death. Not cheerlessly, more and more faintly, her thread of life ran to pause, resembling a rill of the drought; and the thinner-it grew, the shrewder were her murmurs for Carinthia's ears in commending 'the most real of husbands of an unreal wife' to her friendly care of him when he would no longer see the shadow he had wedded. She had the privilege of a soul beyond our minor rules and restrainings to speak her wishes to the true wife of a mock husband- no husband; less a husband than this shadow of a woman a wife, she said; and spoke them without adjuring the bowed head beside her to record a promise or seem to show the far willingness, but merely that the wishes should be heard on earth in her last breath, for a good man's remaining one chance of happiness. On the theme touching her husband Owain, it was verily to hear a soul speak, and have knowledge of the broader range, the rich interflowings of the tuned discords, a spirit past the flesh can find. Her mind was at the same time alive to our worldly conventions when other people came under its light; she sketched them and their views in her brief words between the gasps, with perspicuous, humorous bluntness, as vividly as her twitched eyebrows indicated the laugh. Gower Woodseer she read startlingly, if correctly.

Carinthia could not leave her. Attendance upon this dying woman was a drinking at the springs of life.

Rebecca Wythan under earth, the earl was briefly informed of Lady Fleetwood's consent to quit Wales, obedient to a summons two months old, —and that she would be properly escorted; for the which her lord had made provision. Consequently the tyrant swallowed his wrath, little conceiving the monstrous blow she was about to strike.

In peril of fresh floods from our Dame, who should be satisfied with the inspiring of these pages, it is owned that her story of 'the four and twenty squires of Glamorgan and Caermarthen in their brass-buttoned green coats and buckskins, mounted and armed, an escort of the Countess of Fleetwood across the swollen Severn, along midwinter roads, up to the Kentish gates of Esslemont,' has a foundation, though the story is not the more credible for her flourish of documentary old ballad-sheets, printed when London's wags had ears on cock to any whisper of the doings. of their favourite Whitechapel Countess; and indeed hardly depended on whispers.

Enthusiasm sufficient to troop forth four and twenty and more hundreds of Cambrian gentlemen, and still more of the common folk, as far as they could journey afoot, was over the two halves of the Principality, to give the countess a reputable and gallant body-guard. London had intimations of kindling circumstances concerning her, and magnified them in the interests of the national humour: which is the English way of exalting to criticize, criticizing to depreciate, and depreciating to restore, ultimately to cherish, in reward for the amusement furnished by an eccentric person, not devoid of merit.

These little tales of her, pricking cool blood to some activity, were furze-fires among the Welsh. But where the latter heard Bardic strings inviting a chorus, the former as unanimously obeyed the stroke of their humorous conductor's baton for an outburst from the ribs or below. And it was really funny to hear of Whitechapel's titled heroine roaming Taffyland at her old pranks.

Catching a maddened bull by the horns in the marketplace, and hanging to the infuriate beast, a wild whirl of clouts, till he is reduced to be a subject for steaks, that is no common feat.

Her performances down mines were things of the underworld. England clapped hands, merely objecting to her not having changed her garb for the picador's or matador's, before she seized the bull. Wales adopted and was proud of her in any costume. Welshmen North and South, united for the nonce, now propose her gallantry as a theme to the rival Bards at the next Eisteddfod. She is to sit throned in full assembly, oak leaves and mistletoe interwoven on her head, a white robe and green sash to clothe her, and the vanquished beast's horns on a gilded pole behind the dais; hearing the eulogies respectively interpreted to her by Colonel Fluellen Wythan at one ear, and Captain Agincourt Gower at the other. A splendid scene; she might well insist to be present.

There, however, we are at the pitch of burlesque beyond her illustrious lord's capacity to stand. Peremptory orders from England arrive, commanding her return. She temporizes, postpones, and supplicates to have the period extended up to the close of the Eisteddfod. My lord's orders are imperatively repeated, and very blunt. He will not have her 'continue playing the fool down there.' She holds her ground from August into February, and then sets forth, to undergo the further process of her taming at Esslemont in England; with Llewellyn and Vaughan and Cadwallader, and Watkyn and Shenkyn and the remains of the race of Owen Tudor, attending her; vowed to extract a receipt from the earl her lord's responsible servitors for the safe delivery of their heroine's person at the gates of Esslemont; ich dien their trumpeted motto.

Counting the number at four and twenty, it wears the look of an invasion. But the said number is a ballad number, and has been since the antique time. There was, at a lesser number, enough of a challenge about it for squires of England, never in those days backward to pick up a glove or give the ringing rejoinder for a thumb-bite, to ride out and tilt compliments with the Whitechapel Countess's green cavaliers, rally their sprites and entertain them exactly according to their degrees of dignity, as exhibited by their 'haviour under something of a trial; and satisfy also such temporary appetites as might be excited in them by (among other matters left to the luck of events) a metropolitan play upon the Saxon tongue, hard of understanding to the leeky cocks until their ready store of native pepper seasons it; which may require a corresponding English condiment to rectify the flavour of the stew.

Now the number of Saxe-Normans riding out to meet and greet the Welshmen is declared to have not exceeded nine. So much pretends to be historic, in opposition to the poetic version. They would, we may be sure, have made it a point of honour to meet and greet their invading guests in precisely similar numbers a larger would have overshot the mark of courtesy; and doubtless a smaller have fallen deplorably short of it. Therefore, an acquaintance with her chivalrous, if less impulsive, countrymen compels to the dismissing of the Dame's ballad authorities. She has every right to quote them for her own good pleasure, and may create in others an enjoyment of what has been called 'the Mackrell fry.'

Her notion of a ballad is, that it grows like mushrooms from a scuffle of feet on grass overnight, and is a sort of forest mother of the pied infant reared and trimmed by historians to show the world its fatherly antecedent steps. The hand of Rose Mackrell is at least suggested in more than one of the ballads. Here the Welsh irruption is a Chevy Chase; next we have the countess for a disputed Helen.

The lady's lord is not a shining figure. How can an undecided one be a dispenser of light? Poetry could never allow him to say with her:

> 'Where'er I go I make a name,
> And leave a song to follow.'

Yet he was the master of her fortunes at the time; all the material power was his. Even doggerel verse (it is worth while to brood on the fact) denies a surviving pre-eminence to the potent moody, reverses the position between the driven and the driver. Poetry, however erratic, is less a servant of the bully Present, or pomlious Past, than History. The Muse of History has neither the same divination of the intrinsic nor the devotion to it, though truly, she has possession of all the positive matter and holds us faster by the crediting senses.

Nine English cavaliers, then, left London early on a January or February morning in a Southerly direction, bearing East; and they were the Earl of Fleetwood's intimates, of the half-dependent order; so we may suppose them to have gone at his bidding. That they met the procession of the Welsh, and claimed to take charge of the countess's carriage, near the Kentish border-line, is an assertion supported by testimony fairly acceptable.

Intelligence of the advancing party had reached the earl by courier, from the date of the first gathering on the bridge of Pont-y-pridd; and from Gloucester, along to the Thames at Reading; thence away to the Mole, from Mickleham, where the Surrey chalk runs its final turfy spine North-eastward to the slope upon Kentish soil.

Greatly to the astonishment of the Welsh cavaliers, a mounted footman, clad in the green and scarlet facings of Lord Fleetwood's livery, rode up to them a mile outside the principal towns and named the inn where the earl had ordered preparations for the reception of them. England's hospitality was offered on a princely scale. Cleverer fencing could not be.

The meeting, in no sense an encounter, occurred close by a thirty-acre meadow, famous over the county; and was remarkable for the punctilious exchange of ceremonial speech, danger being present; as we see powder-magazines protected by their walls and fosses and covered alleys. Notwithstanding which, there was a scintillation of sparks.

Lord Brailstone, spokesman of the welcoming party, expressed comic regrets that they had not an interpreter with them.

Mr. Owain Wythan, in the name of the Cambrian chivalry, assured him of their comprehension and appreciation of English slang.

Both gentlemen kept their heads uncovered in a suspense; they might for a word or two more of that savour have turned into the conveniently spacious meadow. They were induced, on the contrary, to enter the channel of English humour, by hearing Chumley Potts exclaim: 'His nob!' and all of them laughed at the condensed description of a good hit back, at the English party's cost.

Laughter, let it be but genuine, is of a common nationality, indeed a common fireside; and profound disagreement is not easy after it. The Dame professes to believe that 'Carinthia Jane' had to intervene as peacemaker, before the united races took the table in Esslemont's dining- hall for a memorable night of it, and a contest nearer the mark of veracity than that shown in another of the ballads she would have us follow. Whatever happened, they sat down at table together, and the point of honour for them each and every was, not to be first to rise from it. Once more the pure Briton and the mixed if not fused English engaged, Bacchus for instrument this time, Bacchus for arbiter of the fray.

You may imagine! says the Dame. She cites the old butler at Esslemont, 'as having been much questioned on the subject by her family relative, Dr. Glossop, and others interested to know the smallest items of the facts,'—and he is her authority for the declaration that the Welsh gentlemen and the English gentlemen, 'whatever their united number,' consumed the number of nine dozen and a half of old Esslemont wine before they rose, or as possibly sank, at the festive board at the hour of five of the morning.

Years later, this butler, Joshua Queeney, 'a much enfeebled old man,' retold and enlarged the tale of the enormous consumption of his best wine; with a sacred oath to confirm it, and a tear expressive of elegiacal feelings.

'They bled me twelve dozen, not a bottle less,' she quotes him, after a minute description of his countenance and scrupulously brushed black suit, pensioner though he had become. He had grown, during the interval, to be more communicative as to particulars. The wines were four. Sherry led off the parade pace, Hock the trot into the merry canter, Champagne the racing gallop, Burgundy the grand trial of constitutional endurance for the enforced finish. All these wines, except the sparkling, had their date of birth in the precedent century. 'They went like water.'

Questioned anxiously by Dr. Glossop, Queeney maintained an impartial attitude, and said there was no victor, no vanquished. They did not sit in blocks. The tactics for preserving peace intermingled them. Each English gentleman had a Welsh gentleman beside him; they both sat firm; both fell together. The bottles or decanters were not stationary for the guest to fill his glass, they circulated, returning to an empty glass. All drank equally. Often the voices were high, the talk was loud. The gentlemen were too serious to sing.

At one moment of the evening Queeney confidently anticipated a 'fracassy,' he said. One of the foreign party—and they all spoke English, after five dozen bottles had gone the round, as correct as the English themselves—remarked on the seventy-years Old Brown Sherry, that 'it had a Madeira flavour.' He spoke it approvingly. Thereupon Lord Simon Pitscrew calls to Queeney, asking him 'why Madeira had been supplied instead of Esslemont's renowned old Sherry?' A second Welsh gentleman gave his assurances that his friend had not said it was Madeira. But Lord Brailstone accused them of the worse unkindness to a venerable Old Brown Sherry, in attributing a Madeira flavour to it. Then another Welsh gentleman briskly and emphatically stated his opinion, that the attribution of Madeira flavour to it was a compliment. At this, which smelt strongly, he said, of insult, Captain Abrane called on the name of their absent host to warrant the demand of an apology to the Old Brown Sherry, for the imputation denying it an individual distinction. Chumley Potts offered generally to bet that he would distinguish blindfold at a single sip any Madeira from any first-class Sherry, Old Brown or Pale. 'Single sip or smell!' Ambrose Mallard cried, either for himself or his comrade, Queeney could not say which.

Of all Lord Fleetwood's following, Mr. Potts and Mr. Mallard were, the Dame informs us, Queeney's favourites, because they were so genial; and he remembered most of what they said and did, being moved to it by 'poor young Mr. Mallard's melancholy end and Mr. Potts's grief!'

The Welsh gentlemen, after paying their devoirs to the countess next morning, rode on in fresh health and spirits at mid-day to Barlings, the seat of Mr. Mason Fennell, a friend of Mr. Owain Wythan's. They shouted, in an unseemly way, Queeney thought, at their breakfast-table, to hear that three of the English party, namely, Captain Abrane, Mr. Mallard, and Mr. Potts, had rung for tea and toast in bed. Lord Simon Pitscrew, Lord Brailstone, and the rest of the English were sore about it; for it certainly wore a look of constitutional inferiority on the English side, which could boast of indubitably stouter muscles. The frenzied spirits of the Welsh gentlemen, when riding off, let it be known what their opinion was. Under the protection of the countess's presence, they were so cheery as to seem triumphantly ironical; they sent messages of condolence to the three in bed.

With an undisguised reluctance, the countess, holding Mr. Owain Wythan's hand longer than was publicly decent, calling him by his Christian name, consented to their departure. As they left, they defiled before her; the vow was uttered by each, that at the instant of her summons he would mount and devote himself to her service, individually or collectively. She waved her hand to them. They ranged in line and saluted. She kissed her hand. Sweeping the cavaliers' obeisance, gallantest of bows, they rode away.

A striking scene, Dame Gossip says; but raises a wind over the clipped adventure, and is for recounting what London believed about it. Enough has been conceded for the stoppage of her intrusion; she is left in the likeness of a full-charged pistol capless to the clapping trigger.

That which London believed, or affected to believe about it, would fill chapters. There was during many months an impression of Lord Fleetwood's countess as of a tenacious, dread, prevailing young woman, both intrepid and astute, who had, by an exercise of various arts, legitimate in open war of husband and wife, gathered the pick of the Principality to storm and carry another of her husband's houses. The certification that her cavaliers were Welsh gentlemen of wealth and position required a broader sneer at the Welsh than was warranted by later and more intimate acquaintance, if it could be made to redound to her discredit. So, therefore, added to the national liking for a plucky woman, she gained the respect for power. Whitechapel was round her like London's one street's length extension of smoky haze, reminder of the morning's fog under novel sunbeams.

Simultaneously, strange to say, her connubial antagonist, far from being overshadowed, grew to be proportionately respected, and on the strength of his deserts, apart from his title and his wealth. He defended himself, as he was bound to do, by welcoming the picked Welsh squires with hospitable embrace, providing ceremonies, receptions, and most comfortable arrangements for them, along the route. But in thus gravely entering into the knightly burlesque of the procession, and assisting to swell the same, he not only drew the venom from it, he stood forth as England's deputed representative, equal to her invasive challengeing guests at all points, comic, tragic, or cordial. He saw that it had to be treated as a national affair; and he parried the imputation which would have injured his country's name for courtly breeding, had they been ill-received, while he rescued his own good name from derision by joining the extravagance.

He was well inspired. It was popularly felt to be the supreme of clever-nay, noble-fencing. Really noble, though the cleverness was conspicuous. A defensive stroke, protecting him against his fair one's violent charge of horse, warded off an implied attack upon Old England, in Old England's best-humoured easy manner.

Supposing the earl to have acted otherwise, his countess would virtually have ridden over him, and wild Wales have cast a shadow on the chivalry of magisterial England. He and his country stood to meet the issue together the moment the Countess of Fleetwood and her escort crossed the Welsh border; when it became a question between the hot-hearted, at their impetuous gallop, and the sedatively minded, in an unfortified camp of arm-chairs. The earl's adroitness, averting a collision fatal or discomforting to both, disengaged him from an incumbent odium, of which, it need hardly be stated, neither the lady nor her attendant cavaliers had any notion at the hour of the assembly for the start for England on the bridge of Pont-y-pridd. The hungry mother had the safety of her babe in thought. The hotheaded Welshmen were sworn to guard their heroine.

That is the case presented by the Dame's papers, when the incredible is excised. She claims the being a good friend to fiction in feeding popular voracity with all her stores. But the Old Buccaneer, no professed friend to it, is a sounder guide in the maxim, where he says: Deliver yourself by permit of your cheque on the 'Bank of Reason, and your account is increased instead of lessened.

Our account with credulity, he would signify.

The Dame does not like the shaking for a sifting. Romance, however, is not a mountain made of gold, but a vein running some way through; and it must be engineered, else either we are filled with wind from swallowing indigestible substance, or we consent to a debasing of the currency, which means her to-morrow's bankruptcy; and the spectacle of Romance in the bankruptcy court degrades us (who believe we are allied to her) as cruelly as it appals. It gives the cynic licence to bark day and night for an entire generation.

Surely the Countess of Fleetwood's drive from the Welsh borders to Esslemont, accompanied by the chosen of the land, followed by the vivats of the whole Principality, and England gaping to hear the stages of her progress, may be held sufficiently romantic without stuffing of surprises and conflicts, adventures at inns, alarms at midnight, windings of a horn over hilly verges of black heaths, and the rape of the child, the pursuit, the recovery of the child, after a new set of heroine performances on the part of a strung-wire mother, whose outcry in a waste country district, as she clasps her boy to her bosom again: 'There's a farm I see for milk for him!' the Dame repeats, having begun with an admission that the tale has been contradicted, and is not produced on authority. The end in design is to win the ear by making a fuss, and roll event upon event for the braining of common intelligence, until her narrative resembles dusty troopings along a road to the races.

Carinthia and her babe reached Esslemont, no matter what impediments. There, like a stopped runner whose pantings lengthen to the longer breath, her alarms over the infant subsided, ceasing for as long as she clasped it or was in the room with it. Walking behind the precious donkey-basket round the park, she went armed, and she soon won a fearful name at Kentish cottage-hearths, though she 'was not black to see, nor old. No, she was very young. But she did all the things that soldiers do,—was a bit of a foreigner;—she brought a reputation up from the Welsh land, and it had a raven's croak and a glow-worm's drapery and a goblin's origin.

Something was hinted of her having agitated London once. Somebody dropped word of her and that old Lord Levellier up at Croridge. She stalked park and country at night. Stories, one or two near the truth, were told of a restless and a very decided lady down these parts as well; and the earl her husband daren't come nigh in his dread of her, so that he runs as if to save his life out of every place she enters. And he's not one to run for a trifle. His pride is pretty well a match for princes and princesses.

All the same, he shakes in his shoes before her, durst hardly spy at Esslemont again while she's in occupation. His managing gentleman comes down from him, and goes up from her; that's how they communicate. One week she's quite solitary; another week the house is brimful as can be. She 's the great lady entertaining then. Yet they say it 's a fact, she has not a shilling of her own to fling at a beggar. She 'll stock a cottage wanting it with provision for a fortnight or more, and she'll order the doctor in, and she'll call and see the right things done for illness. 'But no money; no one's to expect money of her. The shots you hear in Esslemont grounds out of season are she and her maid, always alongside her, at it before a target on a bank, trying that old Lord Levellier's gunpowder out of his mill; and he's got no money either; not for his workmen, they say, until they congregate, and a threatening to blow him up brings forth half their pay, on account. But he 's a known miser. She's not that. She's a pleasant-faced lady for the poor. She has the voice poor people like. It's only her enemy, maybe her husband, she can be terrible to. She'd drive a hole through a robber stopping her on the road, as soon as look at him.

This was Esslemont's atmosphere working its way to the earl, not so very long after the establishment of his countess there. She could lay hold of the English, too, it seemed. Did she call any gentleman of the district by his Christian name? Lord Simon Pitscrew reported her doing so in the case of one of the Welshmen. Those Welshmen! Apparently they are making a push for importance in the kingdom!

CHAPTER XXXV
IN WHICH CERTAIN CHANGES MAY BE DISCERNED

Behind his white plaster of composure, Lord Fleetwood had alternately raged and wondered during the passage of the Welsh cavalcade up Eastward: a gigantic burlesque, that would have swept any husband of their heroine off the scene had he failed to encounter it deferentially, preserving his countenance and ostensibly his temper. An idiot of a woman, incurable in her lunacy, suspects the father of the infant as guilty of designs done to death in romances; and so she manages to set going solemnly a bigger blazing Tom Fool's show than any known or written romance gives word of! And that fellow, Gower Woodseer, pleads, in apology, for her husband's confusion, physiologically, that it comes of her having been carried off and kept a prisoner when she was bearing the child and knitting her whole mind to ensure the child. But what sheer animals these women are, if they take impressions in such a manner! And Mr. Philosopher argues that the abusing of women proves the hating of Nature; names it 'the commonest insanity, and the deadliest,' and men are 'planted in the bog of their unclean animal condition until they do proper homage to the animal Nature makes the woman be.' Oh, pish, sir!—as Meeson Corby had the habit of exclaiming when Abrane's 'fiddler' argues him into a corner. The fellow can fiddle fine things and occasionally clear sense:—'Men hating Nature are insane. Women and Nature are close. If it is rather general to hate Nature and maltreat women, we begin to see why the world is a mad world.' That is the tune of the fiddler's fiddling. As for him, something protects him. He was the slave of Countess Livia; like Abrane, Mallard, Corby, St. Ombre, young Cressett, and the dozens. He is now her master. Can a man like that be foolish, in saying of the Countess Carinthia, she is 'not only quick to understand, she is in the quick of understanding'? Gower Woodseer said it of her in Wales, and again on the day of his walk up to London from Esslemont, after pedestrian exercise, which may heat the frame, but cools the mind. She stamped that idea on a thoughtful fellow.

He's a Welshman. They are all excitable,—have heads on hound's legs for a flying figure in front. Still, they must have an object, definitely seen by them—definite to them if dim to their neighbours; and it will run in the poetic direction: and the woman to win them, win all classes of them, within so short a term, is a toss above extraordinary. She is named Carinthia—suitable name for the Welsh pantomimic procession. Or cry out the word in an amphitheatre of Alpine crags,—it sounds at home.

She is a daughter of the mountains,—should never have left them. She is also a daughter of the Old Buccaneer—no poor specimen of the fighting Englishman of his day. According to Rose Mackrell, he, this Old Buccaneer, it was, who, by strange adventures, brought the great Welsh mines into the family! He would not be ashamed in spying through his nautical glass, up or down, at his daughter's doings. She has not yet developed a taste for the mother's tricks:—the mother, said to have been a kindler. That Countess of Cressett was a romantic little fly-away bird. Both parents were brave: the daughter would inherit gallantry. She inherits a kind of thwarted beauty. Or it needs the situation seen in Wales: her arms up and her unaffrighted eyes over the unappeasable growl. She had then the beauty coming from the fathom depths, with the torch of Life in the jaws of Death to light her: beauty of the nether kingdom mounting to an upper place in the higher. Her beauty recognized, the name of the man who married her is not Longears—not to himself, is the main point; nor will it be to the world when he shows that it is not so to himself.

Suppose he went to her, would she be trying at domination? The woman's pitch above woman's beauty was perceived to be no intermittent beam, but so living as to take the stamp of permanence. More than to say it was hers, it was she. What a deadly peril brought into view was her character-soul, some call it: generally a thing rather distasteful in women, or chilling to the masculine temperament. Here it attracts. Here, strange to say, it is the decided attraction, in a woman of a splendid figure and a known softness. By rights, she should have more understanding than to suspect the husband as guilty of designs done to death in romances. However, she is not a craven who compliments him by rearing him, and he might prove that there is no need for fear. But she would be expecting explanations before the reconcilement. The bosom of these women will keep on at its quick heaving until they have heard certain formal words, oaths to boot. How speak them?

His old road of the ladder appeared to Fleetwood an excellent one for obviating explanations and effecting the reconcilement without any temporary seeming forfeit of the native male superiority. For there she is at Esslemont now; any night the window could be scaled. 'It is my husband.' The soul was in her voice when she said it.

He remembered that it had not ennobled her to him then; had not endeared; was taken for a foreign example of the childish artless, imperfectly suited to our English clime.' The tone of adorable utterances, however much desired, is never for repetition; nor is the cast of divine sweet looks; nor are the particular deeds-once pardonable, fitly pleaded. A second scaling of her window—no, night's black hills girdle the scene with hoarse echoes; the moon rushes out of her clouds grimacing. Even Fleetwood's devil, much addicted to cape and sword and ladder, the vulpine and the gryphine, rejected it.

For she had, by singular transformation since, and in spite of a deluging grotesque that was antecedently incredible, she had become a personage, counting her adherents; she could put half the world in motion on her side. Yell those Welshmen to scorn, they were on a plane finding native ground with as large a body of these English. His baser mind bowed to the fact. Her aspect was entirely different; her attitude toward him as well: insomuch that he had to chain her to her original features by the conjuring of recollected phrases memorable for the vivid portraiture of her foregone simplicity and her devotion to 'my husband.'

Yes, there she was at Essleinont, securely there, near him, to be seen any day; worth claiming, too; a combatant figure, provocative of the fight and the capture rather than repellent. The respect enforced by her attitude awakened in him his inherited keen old relish for our intersexual strife and the indubitable victory of the stronger, with the prospect of slavish charms, fawning submission, marrowy spoil. Or perhaps, preferably, a sullen submission, reluctant charms; far more marrowy. Or who can say?—the creature is a rocket of the shot into the fiery garland of stars; she may personate any new marvel, be an unimagined terror, an overwhelming bewitchment: for she carries the unexpected in her bosom. And does it look like such indubitable victory, when the man, the woman's husband, divided from her, toothsome to the sex, acknowledges within himself and lets the world know his utter dislike of other women's charms, to the degree that herbal anchorites positively could not be colder, could not be chaster: and he no forest bird, but having the garden of the variety of fairest flowers at nod and blush about him! That was the truth. Even Henrietta's beauty had the effect of a princess's birthday doll admired on show by a contemptuous boy.

Wherefore, then, did the devil in him seek to pervert this loveliest of young women and feed on her humiliation for one flashing minute? The taste had gone, the desire of the vengeance was extinct, personal gratification could not exist. He spied into himself, and set it down to one among the many mysteries.

Men uninstructed in analysis of motives arrive at this dangerous conclusion, which spares their pride and caresses their indolence, while it flatters the sense of internal vastness, and invites to headlong intoxication. It allows them to think they are of such a compound, and must necessarily act in that manner. They are not taught at the schools or by the books of the honoured places in the libraries, to examine and see the simplicity of these mysteries, which it would be here and there a saving grace for them to see; as the minstrel, dutifully inclining to the prosy in their behalf and morality's, should exhibit; he should arrest all the characters of his drama to spring it to vision and strike perchance the chord primarily if not continually moving them, that readers might learn the why and how of a germ of evil, its flourishing under rebuke, the persistency of it after the fell creative energy has expired and pleasure sunk to be a phlegmatic dislike, almost a loathing.

This would here be done, but for signs of a barometric dead fall in Dame Gossip's chaps, already heavily pendent. She would be off with us on one of her whirling cyclones or elemental mad waltzes, if a step were taken to the lecturing-desk. We are so far in her hands that we have to keep her quiet. She will not hear of the reasons and the change of reasons for one thing and the other. Things were so: narrate them, and let readers do their reflections for themselves, she says, denouncing our conscientious method as the direct road downward to the dreadful modern appeal to the senses and assault on them for testimony to the veracity of everything described; to the extent that, at the mention of a vile smell, it shall be blown into the reader's nostrils, and corking-pins attack the comfortable seat of him simultaneously with a development of surprises. 'Thither your conscientiousness leads.'

It is not perfectly visible. And she would gain information of the singular nature of the young of the male sex in listening to the wrangle between Lord Fleetwood and Gower Woodseer on the subject of pocket-money for the needs of the Countess Carinthia. For it was a long and an angry one, and it brought out both of them, exposing, of course, the more complex creature the most. They were near a rupture, so scathing was Gower's tone of irate professor to shirky scholar—or it might be put, German professor to English scuffleshoe.

She is for the scene of 'Chillon John's' attempt to restore the respiration of his bank-book by wager; to wit, that he would walk a mile, run a mile, ride a mile, and jump ten hurdles, then score five rifle- shots at a three hundred yards' distant target within a count of minutes; twenty-five, she says; and vows it to have been one of the most exciting of scenes ever witnessed on green turf in the land of wagers; and that he was accomplishing it quite certainly when, at the first of the hurdles, a treacherous unfolding and waving of a white flag caused his horse to swerve and the loss of one minute, seven and twenty seconds, before he cleared the hurdles; after which, he had to fire his shots hurriedly, and the last counted blank, for being outside the circle of the stated time.

So he was beaten. But a terrific uproar over the field proclaimed the popular dissatisfaction. Presently there was a cleavage of the mob, and behold a chase at the heels of the fellow to rival the very captain himself for fleetness. He escaped, leaving his pole with the sheet nailed to it, by way of flag, in proof of foul play; or a proof, as the other side declared, of an innocently premature signalizing of the captain's victory.

However that might be, he ran. Seeing him spin his legs at a hound's pace, half a mile away, four countrymen attempted to stop him. All four were laid on their backs in turn with stupefying celerity; and on rising to their feet, and for the remainder of their natural lives, they swore that no man but a Champion could have floored them so. This again may have been due to the sturdy island pride of four good men knocked over by one. We are unable to decide. Wickedness there was, the Dame says; and she counsels the world to 'put and put together,' for, at any rate, 'a partial elucidation of a most mysterious incident.' As to the wager- money, the umpires dissented; a famous quarrel, that does not concern us here, sprang out of the dispute; which was eventually, after great disturbance 'of the country, referred to three leading sportsmen in the metropolitan sphere, who pronounced the wager 'off,' being two to one. Hence arose the dissatisfied third party, and the letters of this minority to the newspapers, exciting, if not actually dividing, all England for several months.

Now the month of December was the month of the Dame's mysterious incident. From the date of January, as Madge Winch knew, Christopher Ines had ceased to be in the service of the Earl of Fleetwood. At Esslemont Park gates, one winter afternoon of a North-east wind blowing 'rum-shrub into men for a stand against rheumatics,' as he remarked, Ines met the girl by appointment, and informing her that he had money, and that Lord Fleetwood was 'a black nobleman,' he proposed immediate marriage. The hymeneal invitation, wafted to her on the breath of rum- shrub, obtained no response from Madge until she had received evasive answers as to why the earl dismissed him, and whence the stock of money came.

Lord Fleetwood, he repeated, was a black nobleman. She brought him to say of his knowledge, that Lord Fleetwood hated, and had reason to hate, Captain Levellier. 'Shouldn't I hate the man took my sweetheart from me and popped me into the noose with his sister instead?' Madge was now advised to be overcome by the smell of rum-shrub:—a mere fancy drink tossed off by heroes in their idle moments, before they settle down to the serious business of real drinking, Kit protested. He simulated envious admiration of known heroes, who meant business, and scorned any of the weak stuff under brandy, and went at it till the bottles were the first to give in. For why? They had to stomach an injury from the world or their young woman, and half-way on they shoved that young person and all enemies aside, trampled 'em. That was what Old O'Devy signified; and many's the man driven to his consolation by a cat of a girl, who's like the elements in their puffs and spits at a gallant ship, that rides the tighter and the tighter for all they can do to capsize. 'Tighter than ever I was tight I'll be to-night, if you can't behave.'

They fell upon the smack of words. Kit hitched and huffed away, threatening bottles. Whatever he had done, it was to establish the petticoated hornet in the dignity of matron of a champion light-weight's wholesome retreat of a public-house. A spell of his larkish hilarity was for the punishment of the girl devoted to his heroical performances, as he still considered her to be, though women are notoriously volatile, and her language was mounting a stage above the kitchen.

Madge had little sorrow for him. She was the girl of the fiery heart, not the large heart; she could never be devoted to more than one at a time, and her mistress had all her heart. In relation to Kit, the thought of her having sacrificed her good name to him, flung her on her pride of chastity, without the reckoning of it as a merit. It was the inward assurance of her independence: the young spinster's planting of the, standard of her proud secret knowledge of what she is, let it be a thing of worth or what you will, or the world think as it may. That was her thought.

Her feeling, the much livelier animation, was bitter grief, because her mistress, unlike herself, had been betrayed by her ignorance of the man into calling him husband. Just some knowledge of the man! The warning to the rescue might be there. For nothing did the dear lady weep except for her brother's evil fortune. The day when she had intelligence from Mrs. Levellier of her brother's defeat, she wept over the letter on her knees long hours. 'Me, my child, my brother!' she cried more than once. She had her suspicion of the earl then, and instantly, as her loving servant had. The suspicion was now no dark light, but a clear day-beam to Madge. She adopted Kit's word of Lord Fleetwood. 'A black nobleman he is! he is!' Her mistress had written like a creature begging him for money. He did not deign a reply. To her! When he had seen good proof she was the bravest woman on earth; and she rushed at death to save a child, a common child; as people say. And who knows but she saved that husband of hers, too, from bites might have sent him out of the world barking, and all his wealth not able to stop him!

They were in the month of March. Her dear mistress had been begging my lord through Mr. Woodseer constantly of late for an allowance of money; on her knees to him, as it seemed; and Mr. Woodseer was expected at Esslemont. Her mistress was looking for him eagerly. Something her heart was in depended on it, and only her brother could be the object, for now she loved only him of these men; though a gentleman coming over from Barlings pretty often would pour mines of money into her lap for half a word.

Carinthia had walked up to Croridge in the morning to meet her brother at Lekkatts. Madge was left guardian of the child. She liked a stroll any day round Esslemont Park, where her mistress was beginning to strike roots; as she soon did wherever she was planted, despite a tone of pity for artificial waters and gardeners' arts. Madge respected them. She knew nothing of the grandeur of wildness. Her native English veneration for the smoothing hand of wealth led her to think Esslemont the home of all homes for a lady with her husband beside her. And without him, too, if he were wafted over seas and away: if there would but come a wind to do that!

> The wild North-easter tore the budded beeches. Master John Edward Russett lay in the cradling-basket drawn by his docile donkey, Martha and Madge to right and left of him; a speechless rustic, graduating in footman's livery, to rear.

At slow march round by the wrinkled water, Madge saw the park gates flung wide. A coach drove up the road along on the farther rim of the circle, direct for the house. It stopped, the team turned leisurely and came at a smart pace toward the carriage-basket. Lord Fleetwood was recognized.

He alighted, bidding one of his grooms drive to stables. Madge performed her reverence, aware that she did it in clumsy style; his presence had startled her instincts and set them travelling.

'Coldish for the youngster,' he said. 'All well, Madge?'

> 'Baby sleeps in the air, my lord,' she replied. 'My lady has gone to Croridge.'

'Sharp air for a child, isn't it?'

'My lady teaches him to breathe with his mouth shut, like her father taught her when she was little. Our baby never catches colds.'

Madge displayed the child's face.

The father dropped a glance on it from the height of skies.

'Croridge, you said?'

'Her uncle, Lord Levellier's.'

'You say, never catches cold?'

'Not our baby, my lord.'

Probably good management on the part of the mother. But the wife's absence disappointed the husband strung to meet her, and an obtrusion of her practical motherhood blurred the prospect demanded by his present step.

'When do you expect her to return, Madge?'

'Before nightfall, my lord.'

'She walks?'

'Oh yes, my lady is fond of walking.'

'I suppose she could defend herself?'

'My lady walks with a good stick.'

Fleetwood weighed the chances; beheld her figure attacked, Amazonian.

'And tell me, my dear—Kit?'

I don't see more of Kit Ines.'

'What has the fellow done?'

'I'd like him to let me know why he was dismissed.'

'Ah. He kept silent on that point.'

'He let out enough.'

'You've punished him, if he's to lose a bonny
sweetheart, poor devil!
Your sister Sally sends you messages?'

'We're both of us grateful, my lord.'

He lifted the thin veil from John Edward Russett's face with a loveless hand.

'You remember the child bitten by a dog down in Wales. I have word from my manager there. Poor little wretch has died—died raving.'

Madge's bosom went shivering up and sank. 'My lady was right. She's not often wrong.'

'She's looking well?' said the earl, impatient with her moral merits:—and this communication from Wales had been the decisive motive agent in hurrying him at last to Esslemont. The next moment he heard coolly of the lady's looking well. He wanted fervid eulogy of his wife's looks, if he was to hear any.

CHAPTER XXXVI
BELOW THE SURFACE AND ABOVE

The girl was counselled by the tremor of her instincts to forbear to speak of the minor circumstance, that her mistress had, besides a good stick, a good companion on the road to Croridge: and she rejoiced to think her mistress had him, because it seemed an intimation of justice returning upon earth. She was combative, a born rebel against tyranny. She weighed the powers, she felt to the worth of the persons coming into her range of touch: she set her mistress and my lord fronting for a wrestle, and my lord's wealth went to thin vapour, and her mistress's character threw him. More dimly, my lord and the Welsh gentleman were put to the trial: a tough one for these two men. She did not proclaim the winner, but a momentary flutter of pity in the direction of Lord Fleetwood did as much. She pitied him; for his presence at Esslemont betrayed an inclination; he was ignorant of his lady's character, of how firm she could be to defy him and all the world, in her gratitude to the gentleman she thought of as her true friend, smiled at for his open nature,—called by his Christian name.

The idea of a piece of information stinging Lord Fleetwood, the desire to sting, so as to be an instrument of retribution (one of female human nature's ecstasies); and her, abstaining, that she, might not pain the lord who had been generous to her sister Sally, made the force in Madge's breast which urges to the gambling for the undeveloped, entitled prophecy. She kept it low and felt it thrill.

Lord Fleetwood, chatted; Madge had him wincing. He might pull the cover off the child's face carelessly—he looked at the child. His look at the child was a thought of the mother. If he thought of the mother, he would be wanting to see her. If he heard her call a gentleman by his Christian name, and heard the gentleman say 'Carinthia' my lord would begin to shiver at changes. Women have to do unusual things when they would bring that outer set to human behaviour. Perhaps my lord would mount the coach-box and whip his horses away, adieu forever. His lady would not weep. He might, perhaps, command her to keep her mouth shut from gentlemen's Christian names, all except his own. His lady would not obey. He had to learn something of changes that had come to others as well as to himself. Ah, and then would he dare hint, as base men will? He may blow foul smoke on her, she will shine out of it. He has to learn what she is, that is his lesson; and let him pray all night and work hard all day for it not to be too late. Let him try to be a little like Mr. Woodseer, who worships the countess, and is hearty with the gentleman she treats as her best of friends. There is the real nobleman.

Fleetwood chatted on airily. His instincts were duller than those of the black-browed girl, at whom he gazed for idle satisfaction of eye from time to time while she replied demurely and maintained her drama of, the featureless but well-distinguished actors within her bosom,—a round, plump bust, good wharfage and harbourage, he was thinking. Excellent harbourage, supposing the arms out in pure good-will. A girl to hold her voyager fast and safe! Men of her class had really a capital choice in a girl like this. Men of another class as well, possibly, for temporary anchorage out midchannel. No?—possibly not. Here and there a girl is a Tartar. Ines talked of her as if she were a kind of religious edifice and a doubt were sacrilege. She could impress the rascal: girls have their arts for reaching the holy end, and still they may have a welcome for a foreign ship.

The earl said humorously: 'You will grant me permission to lunch at your mistress's table in her absence?' And she said: 'My lord!' And he resumed, to waken her interest with a personal question: 'You like our quiet country round Esslemont?' She said: 'I do,' and gave him plain look for look. Her eye was undefended: he went into it, finding neither shallow nor depth, simply the look, always the look; whereby he knew that no story of man was there, and not the shyest of remote responsive invitations from Nature's wakened and detected rogue. The bed of an unmarried young woman's eye yields her secret of past and present to the intrepid diver, if he can get his plunge; he holds her for the tenth of a minute, that is the revealment. Jewel or oyster-shell, it is ours. She cannot withhold it, he knew right well. This girl, then, was, he could believe, one of the rarely exampled innocent in knowledge. He was practised to judge.

Invitation or challenge or response from the handsomest he would have scorned just then. His native devilry suffered a stir at sight of an innocent in knowledge and spotless after experiences. By a sudden singular twist, rather unfairly, naturally, as it happened, he attributed it to an influence issuing from her mistress, to whom the girl was devoted, whom consequently she copied; might physically, and also morally, at a distance, resemble.

'Well, you've been a faithful servant to your lady, my dear; I hope you'll be comfortable here,' he said. 'She likes the mountains.'

'My lady would be quite contented if she could pass two months of the year in the mountains,' Madge answered.

'Look at me. They say people living together get a likeness to one another. What's your opinion? Upon my word, your eyebrows remind me, though they're not the colour—they have a bend!'

'You've seen my lady in danger, my lord.'

'Yes; well, there 's no one to resemble her there, she has her mark—kind of superhuman business. We're none of us "fifty feet high, with phosphorus heads," as your friend Mr. Gower Woodseer says of the prodigiosities. Lady Fleetwood is back—when?'

'Before dark, she should be.'

He ran up the steps to the house.

At Lekkatts beneath Croridge a lean midday meal was being finished hard on the commencement by a silent company of three. When eating is choking to the younger members of the repast, bread and cold mutton-bone serve the turn as conclusively as the Frenchman's buffet-dishes. Carinthia's face of unshed tears dashed what small appetite Chillon had. Lord Levellier plied his fork in his right hand ruminating, his back an arch across his plate.

Riddles to the thwarted young, these old people will not consent to be read by sensations. Carinthia watched his jaws at their work of eating under his victim's eye-knowing Chillon to be no longer an officer in the English service; knowing that her beloved had sold out for the mere money to pay debts and support his Henrietta; knowing, as he must know, that Chillon's act struck a knife to pierce his mother's breast through her coffin-boards! This old man could eat, and he could withhold the means due to his dead sister's son. Could he look on Chillon and not feel that the mother's heart was beating in her son's fortunes? Half the money due to Chillon would have saved him from ruin.

Lord Levellier laid his fork on the plate. He munched his grievance with his bit of meat. The nephew and niece here present feeding on him were not so considerate as the Welsh gentleman, a total stranger, who had walked up to Lekkatts with the Countess of Fleetwood, and expressed the preference to feed at an inn. Relatives are cormorants.

His fork on his plate released the couple. Barely half a dozen words, before the sitting to that niggard restoration, had informed Carinthia of the step taken by her brother. She beckoned him to follow her.

'The worst is done now, Chillon. I am silent. Uncle is a rock. You say we must not offend. I have given him my whole mind. Say where Riette is to live.'

'Her headquarters will be here, at a furnished house. She's, with her cousin, the Dowager.'

'Yes. She should be with me.'

'She wants music. She wants—poor girl! let her have what comes to her.'

Their thoughts beneath their speech were like fish darting under shadow of the traffic bridge.

'She loves music,' said Carinthia; 'it is almost life to her, like fresh air to me. Next month I am in London; Lady Arpington is kind. She will give me as much of their polish as I can take. I dare say I should feel the need of it if I were an enlightened person.'

> 'For instance, did I hear "Owain," when your Welsh
> friend was leaving?'
> Chillon asked.

'It was his dying wife's wish, brother.'

'Keep to the rules, dear.'

'They have been broken, Chillon.'

'Mend them.'

'That would be a step backward.'

'"The right one for defence!" father says.'

'Father says, "The habit of the defensive paralyzes will."'

> '"Womanizes," he says, Carin. You quote him falsely, to
> shield the sex.
> Quite right. But my sister must not be tricky. Keep to the
> rules.
> You're an exceptional woman, and it would be a good
> argument, if you were not in an exceptional position.'

'Owain is the exceptional man, brother.'

'My dear, after all, you have a husband.'

'I have a brother, I have a friend, I have no—I am a man's wife and the mother of his child; I am free, or husband would mean dungeon. Does my brother want an oath from me? That I can give him.'

'Conduct, yes; I couldn't doubt you,' said Chillon. 'But "the world's a flood at a dyke for women, and they must keep watch," you've read.'

'But Owain is not our enemy,' said Carinthia, in her deeper tones, expressive of conviction, and not thereby assuring to hear. 'He is a man with men, a child with women. His Rebecca could describe him; I laugh now at some of her sayings of him; I see her mouth, so tenderly comical over her big "simpleton," she called him, and loved him so.'

The gentleman appeared on the waste land above the house. His very loose black suit and a peculiar roll of his gait likened him to a mourning boatswain who was jolly. In Lord Levellier's workshop his remarks were to the point. Chillon's powders for guns and blasting interested him, and he proposed to ride over from Barlings to witness a test of them.

'You are staying at Barlings?' Chillon said.

'Yes; now Carinthia is at Esslemont,' he replied, astoundingly the simpleton.

His conversation was practical and shrewd on the walk with Chillon and Carinthia down to Esslemont evidently he was a man well armed to encounter the world; social usages might be taught him. Chillon gained a round view of the worthy simple fellow, unlikely to turn out impracticable, for he talked such good sense upon matters of business.

Carinthia saw her brother tickled and interested. A feather moved her. Full of tears though she was, her, heart lay open to the heavens and their kind, small, wholesome gifts. Her happiness in the walk with her brother and her friend—the pair of them united by her companionship, both of them showing they counted her their comrade—was the nearest to the radiant day before she landed on an island, and imagined happiness grew here, and found it to be gilt thorns, loud mockery. A shaving North-easter tore the scream from hedges and the roar from copses under a faceless breadth of sky, and she said, as they turned into Esslemont Park lane: 'We have had one of our old walks to-day, Chillon!'

> 'You used to walk together long walks over in your own country,' said Mr. Wythan.

'Yes, Owain, we did, and my brother never knew me tired.'

'Never knew you confess to it,' said Chillon, as he swallowed the name on her lips.

'Walking was flying over there, brother.'

'Say once or twice in Wales, too,' Mr. Wythan begged of her.

'Wales reminded. Yes, ..Owain, I shall not forget Wales, Welsh people. Mr. Woodseer says they have the three-stringed harp in their breasts, and one string is always humming, whether you pull it or no.'

'That 's love of country! that 's their love of wild Wales, Carinthia.'

There was a quiet interrogation in Chillon's turn of the head at this fervent simpleton.

'I love them for that hum,' said she. 'It joins one in me.'

'Call to them any day, they are up, ready to march!'

'Oh, dear souls!' Carinthia said.

Her breath drew in.

The three were dumb. They saw Lord Fleetwood standing in the park gateway.

CHAPTER XXXVII BETWEEN CARINTHIA AND HER LORD

The earl's easy grace of manner was a ceremonial mantle on him as he grasped the situation in a look. He bent with deferential familiarity to his countess, exactly toning the degree of difference which befitted a salute to the two gentlemen, amiable or hostile.

'There and back?' he said, and conveyed a compliment to Carinthia's pedestrian vigour in the wary smile which can be recalled for a snub.

She replied: 'We have walked the distance, my lord.'

Her smile was the braced one of an untired stepper.

'A cold wind for you.'

'We walked fast.'

She compelled him to take her in the plural, though he addressed her separately, but her tones had their music.

'Your brother, Captain Kirby-Levellier, I believe?'

'My brother is not of the army now, my lord.'

She waved her hand for Madge to conduct donkey and baby to the house. He noticed. He was unruffled.

The form of amenity expected from her, in relation to her brother, was not exhibited. She might perhaps be feeling herself awkward at introductions, and had to be excused.

'I beg,' he said, and motioned to Chillon the way of welcome into the park, saw the fixed figure, and passed over the unspoken refusal, with a remark to Mr. Wythan: 'At Barlings, I presume?'

'My tent is pitched there,' was the answer.

'Good-bye, my brother,' said Carinthia.

Chillon folded his arms round her. 'God bless you, dear love. Let me see you soon.' He murmured:

'You can protect yourself.'

'Fear nothing for me, dearest.'

She kissed her brother's cheek. The strain of her spread fingers on his shoulder signified no dread at her being left behind.

Strangers observing their embrace would have vowed that the pair were brother and sister, and of a notable stock.

'I will walk with you to Croridge again when you send word you are willing to go; and so, good-bye, Owain,' she said.

She gave her hand; frankly she pressed the Welshman's, he not a whit behind her in frankness.

Fleetwood had a skimming sense of a drop upon a funny, whirly world. He kept from giddiness, though the whirl had lasted since he beheld the form of a wild forest girl, dancing, as it struck him now, over an abyss, on the plumed shoot of a stumpy tree.

Ay, and she danced at the ducal schloss;—she mounted his coach like a witch of the Alps up crags;—she was beside him pelting to the vale under a leaden Southwester;—she sat solitary by the fireside in the room of the inn.

Veil it. He consented to the veil he could not lift. He had not even power to try, and his heart thumped.

London's Whitechapel Countess glided before him like a candle in the fog.

He had accused her as the creature destroying Romance. Was it gold in place of gilding, absolute upper human life that the ridiculous object at his heels over London proposed instead of delirious brilliancies, drunken gallops, poison-syrups,—puffs of a young man's vapours?

There was Madge and the donkey basket-trap ahead on the road to the house, bearing proof of the veiled had-been: signification of a might- have-been. Why not a possible might-be? Still the might-be might be. Looking on this shaven earth and sky of March with the wrathful wind at work, we know that it is not the end: a day follows for the world. But looking on those blown black funeral sprays, and the wrinkled chill waters, and the stare of the Esslemont house-windows, it has an appearance of the last lines of our written volume: dead Finis. Not death; fouler, the man alive seeing himself stretched helpless for the altering of his deeds; a coffin carrying him; the fatal whiteheaded sacerdotal official intoning his aims on the march to front, the drear craped files of the liveried, salaried mourners over his failure, trooping at his heels.

Frontward was the small lake's grey water, rearward an avenue of limes.

But the man alive, if but an inch alive, can so take his life in his clutch, that he does alter, cleanse, recast his deeds:—it is known; priests proclaim it, philosophers admit it.

Can he lay his clutch on another's life, and wring out the tears shed, the stains of the bruises, recollection of the wrongs?

Contemplate the wounded creature as a woman. Then, what sort of woman is she? She was once under a fascination—ludicrously, painfully, intensely like a sort of tipsy poor puss, the trapped hare tossed to her serpent; and thoroughly reassured for a few caresses, quite at home, caged and at home; and all abloom with pretty ways, modest pranks, innocent fondlings. Gobbled, my dear!

It is the doom of the innocents, a natural fate. Smother the creature with kindness again, show we are a point in the scale above that old coiler snake—which broke no bones, bit not so very deep;—she will be, she ought to be, the woman she was. That is, if she was then sincere, a dose of kindness should operate happily to restore the honeymoony fancies, hopes, trusts, dreams, all back, as before the honeymoon showed the silver crook and shadowy hag's back of a decaying crescent. And true enough, the poor girl's young crescent of a honeymoon went down sickly- yellow rather early. It can be renewed. She really was at that time rather romantic. She became absurd. Romance is in her, nevertheless. She is a woman of mettle: she is probably expecting to be wooed. One makes a hash of yesterday's left dish, but she may know no better. 'Add a pickle,' as Chummy Potts used to say. The dish is rendered savoury by a slight expenditure of attentions, just a dab of intimated soft stuff.

'Pleasant to see you established here, if you find the place agreeable,' he said.

She was kissing her hand to her brother, all her eyes for him—or for the couple; and they were hidden by the park lodge before she replied: 'It is an admired, beautiful place.'

'I came,' said he, 'to have your assurance that it suits you.'

'I thank you, my lord.'

'"My lord" would like a short rest, Carinthia.'

She seemed placidly acquiescing. 'You have seen the boy?'

'Twice to-day. We were having a conversation just now.'

'We think him very intelligent.'

'Lady Arpington tells me you do the honours here excellently.'

'She is good to me.'

'Praises the mother's management of the young one. John Edward: Edward for call-name. Madge boasts his power for sleeping.'

'He gives little trouble.'

'And babes repay us! We learn from small things. Out of the mouth of babes wisdom? Well, their habits show the wisdom of the mother. A good mother! There's no higher title. A lady of my acquaintance bids fair to win it, they say.'

Carinthia looked in simplicity, saw herself, and said 'If a mother may rear her boy till he must go to school, she is rewarded for all she does.'

'Ah,' said he, nodding over her mania of the perpetual suspicion.
'Leddings, Queeney, the servants here, run smoothly?'

'They do: they are happy in serving.'

'You see, we English are not such bad fellows when we're known. The climate to-day, for example, is rather trying.'

'I miss colours most in England,' said Carinthia. 'I like the winds.
Now and then we have a day to remember.'

'We 're to be "the artist of the day," Gower Woodseer says, and we get an attachment to the dreariest; we are to study "small variations of the commonplace"—dear me! But he may be right. The "sky of lead and scraped lead" over those lines, he points out; and it's not a bad trick for reconciling us to gloomy English weather. You take lessons from him?'

'I can always learn from him,' said Carinthia.

Fleetwood depicted his plodding Gower at the tussle with account-books. She was earnest in sympathy; not awake to the comical; dull as the clouds, dull as the discourse. Yet he throbbed for being near her took impression of her figure, the play of her features, the carriage of her body.

He was shut from her eyes. The clear brown eyes gave exchange of looks; less of admission than her honest maid's.

Madge and the miracle infant awaited them on the terrace. For so foreign did the mother make herself to him, that the appearance of the child, their own child, here between them, was next to miraculous; and the mother, who might well have been the most astonished, had transparently not an idea beyond the verified palpable lump of young life she lifted in her arms out of the arms of Madge, maternally at home with its presence on earth.

Demonstrably a fine specimen, a promising youngster. The father was allowed to inspect him. This was his heir: a little fellow of smiles, features, puckered brows of inquiry; seeming a thing made already, and active on his own account.

'Do people see likenesses?' he asked.

'Some do,' said the mother.

'You?'

She was constrained to give answer. 'There is a likeness to my father, I have thought.'

There's a dotage of idolatrous daughters, he could have retorted; and his gaze was a polite offer to humdrum reconcilement, if it pleased her.

She sent the child up the steps.

'Do you come in, my lord?'

'The house is yours, my lady.'

'I cannot feel it mine.'

'You are the mistress to invite or exclude.'

'I am ready to go in a few hours for a small income of money, for my child and me.'

'—Our child.'

'Yes.'

'It is our child.'

'It is.'

'Any sum you choose to name. But where would you live?'

'Near my brother I would live.'

> 'Three thousand a year for pin-money, or more, are at
> your disposal.
> Stay here, I beg. You have only to notify your wants.
> And we'll talk familiarly now, as we're together. Can I
> be of aid to your brother?
> Tell me, pray. I am disposed in every way to subscribe
> to your wishes.
> Pray, speak, speak out.'

So the earl said. He had to force his familiar tone against the rebuke of her grandeur of stature; and he was for inducing her to deliver her mind, that the mountain girl's feebleness in speech might reinstate him. She rejoined unhesitatingly: 'My brother would not accept aid from you, my lord. I will take no money more than for my needs.'

'You spoke of certain sums down in Wales.'

'I did then.' Her voice was dead.

'Ah! You must be feeling the cold North-wind here.'

'I do not. You may feel the cold, my lord. Will you enter the house?'

' Do you invite me?'

'The house is your own.'

'Will the mistress of the house honour me so far?'

'I am not the mistress of the house, my lord.'

'You refuse, Carinthia?'

'I would keep from using those words. I have no right to refuse the entry of the house to you.'

'If I come in?'

'I guard my rooms.'

She had been awake, then, to the thrusting and parrying behind masked language.

'Good. You are quite decided, I may suppose.'

'I will leave them when I have a little money, or when I know of how I may earn some.'

'The Countess of Fleetwood earning a little money?'

'I can put aside your title, my lord.'

'No, you can't put it aside while the man with the title lives, not even if you're running off in earnest, under a dozen Welsh names. Why should you desire to do it? The title entitles you to the command of half my possessions. As to the house; don't be alarmed; you will not have to guard your rooms. The extraordinary wild animal you—the impression may have been produced; I see, I see. If I were in the house, I should not be rageing at your doors; and it is not my intention to enter the house. That is, not by right of ownership. You have my word.'

He bowed to her, and walked to the stables.

She had the art of extracting his word from him. The word given, she went off with it, disengaged mistress of Esslemont. And she might have the place for residence, but a decent courtesy required that she should remain at the portico until he was out of sight. She was the first out of sight, rather insolently.

She returned him without comment the spell he had cast on her, and he was left to estimate the value of a dirited piece of metal not in the currency, stamped false coin. An odd sense of impoverishment chilled him. Chilly weather was afflicting the whole country, he was reminded, and he paced about hurriedly until his horses were in the shafts. After all, his driving away would be much more expected of him than a stay at the house where the Whitechapel Countess resided, chill, dry, talking the language of early Exercises in English, suitable to her Welshmen. Did she 'Owain' them every one?

As he whipped along the drive and left that glassy stare of Esslemont behind him, there came a slap of a reflection:—here, on the box of this coach, the bride just bursting her sheath sat, and was like warm wax to take impressions. She was like hard stone to retain them, pretty evidently. Like women the world over, she thinks only of her side of the case. Men disdain to plead theirs. Now money is offered her, she declines it. Formerly, she made it the principal subject of her conversation.

Turn the mind to something brighter. Fleetwood strung himself to do so, and became agitated by the question whether the bride sat to left or to right of him when the South-wester blew-a wind altogether preferable to the chill North-east. Women, when they are no longer warm, are colder than the deadliest catarrh wind scything across these islands. Of course she sat to left of him. In the line of the main road, he remembered a look he dropped on her, a look over his left shoulder.

She never had a wooing: she wanted it, had a kind of right to it, or the show of it. How to begin? But was she worth an effort? Turn to something brighter. Religion is the one refuge from women, Feltre says: his Roman Catholic recipe. The old shoemaker, Mr. Woodseer, hauls women into his religion, and purifies them by the process,—fancies he does. He gets them to wear an air. Old Gower, too, has his Religion of Nature, with free admission for women, whom he worships in similes, running away from them, leering sheepishly. No, Feltre's' rigid monastic system is the sole haven. And what a world, where we have no safety except in renouncing it! The two sexes created to devour one another must abjure their sex before they gain 'The Peace,' as Feltre says, impressively, if absurdly. He will end a monk if he has the courage of his logic. A queer spectacle—an English nobleman a shaven monk!

Fleetwood shuddered. We are twisted face about to discover our being saved by women from that horror—the joining the ranks of the nasal friars. By what women? Bacchante, clearly, if the wife we have is a North-easter to wither us, blood, bone, and soul.

He was hungry; he waxed furious with the woman who had flung him out upon the roads. He was thirsty as well. The brightest something to refresh his thoughts grew and glowed in the form of a shiny table, bearing tasty dishes, old wines; at an inn or anywhere. But, out of London, an English inn to furnish the dishes and the wines for a civilized and self- respecting man is hard to seek, as difficult to find as a perfect skeleton of an extinct species. The earl's breast howled derision of his pursuit when he drew up at the; sign of the Royal Sovereign, in the dusky hour, and handed himself desperately to Mrs. Rundles' mercy.

He could not wait for a dinner, so his eating was cold meat. Warned by a sip, that his drinking, if he drank, was to be an excursion in chemical acids, the virtues of an abstainer served for his consolation. Tolerant of tobacco, although he did not smoke, he fronted the fire, envying Gower Woodseer the contemplative pipe, which for half a dozen puffs wafted him to bracing deserts, or primaeval forests, or old highways with the swallow thoughts above him, down the Past, into the Future. A pipe is pleasant dreams at command. A pipe is the concrete form of philosophy. Why, then, a pipe is the alternative of a friar's frock for an escape from women. But if one does not smoke! . . . Here and there a man is visibly in the eyes of all men cursed: let him be blest by Fortune; let him be handsome, healthy, wealthy, courted, he is cursed.

Fleetwood lay that night beneath the roof of the Royal Sovereign. Sleep is life's legitimate mate. It will treat us at times as the faithless wife, who becomes a harrying beast, behaves to her lord. He had no sleep. Having put out his candle, an idea took hold of him, and he jumped up to light it again and verify the idea that this room . . . He left the bed and strode round it, going in the guise of an urgent somnambulist, or ghost bearing burden of an imperfectly remembered mission. This was the room.

Reason and cold together overcame his illogical scruples to lie down on that bed soliciting the sleep desired. He lay and groaned, lay and rolled. All night the Naval Monarch with the loose cheeks and jelly smile of the swinging sign-board creaked. Flaws of the North-easter swung and banged him. He creaked high, in complaint,—low, in some partial contentment. There was piping of his boatswain, shrill piping —shrieks of the whistle. How many nights had that most ill-fated of brides lain listening to the idiotic uproar! It excused a touch of craziness. But how many? Not one, not two, ten, twenty:—count, count to the exact number of nights the unhappy girl must have heard those mad colloquies of the hurricane boatswain and the chirpy king. By heaven! Whitechapel, after one night of it, beckons as a haven of grace.

CHAPTER XXXVIII
A DIP INTO THE SPRING'S WATERS

The night Lord Fleetwood had passed cured him of the wound Carinthia dealt, with her blunt, defensive phrase and her Welshman. Seated on his coach-box, he turned for a look the back way leading to Esslemont, and saw rosed crag and mountain forest rather than the soft undulations of parkland pushing green meadows or brown copse up the slopes under his eye. She had never been courted: she deserved a siege. She was a daughter of the racy highlands. And she, who could say to her husband, 'I guard my rooms,' without sign of the stage-face of scorn or defiance or flinging of the glove, she would have to be captured by siege, it was clear. She wore an aspect of the confident fortress, which neither challenges nor cries to treat, but commands respect. How did she accomplish this miracle of commanding respect after such a string of somersaults before the London world?

He had to drive North-westward: his word was pledged to one of his donkey Ixionides—Abrane, he recollected—to be a witness at some contemptible exhibition of the fellow's muscular skill: a match to punt against a Thames waterman: this time. Odd how it should come about that the giving of his word forced him now to drive away from the woman once causing him to curse his luck as the prisoner of his word! However, there was to be an end of it soon—a change; change as remarkable as Harry Monmouth's at the touching of his crown. Though in these days, in our jog-trot Old England, half a step on the road to greatness is the utmost we can hop; and all England jeers at the man attempting it. He caps himself with this or that one of their titles. For it is not the popular thing among Englishmen. Their hero, when they have done their fighting, is the wealthy patron of Sport. What sort of creatures are his comrades? But he cannot have comrades unless he is on the level of them. Yet let him be never so high above them, they charge him and point him as a piece of cannon; assenting to the flatteries they puff into him, he is their engine. 'The idol of the hour is the mob's wooden puppet, and the doing of the popular thing seed of no harvest,' Gower Woodseer says, moderately well, snuffing incense of his happy delivery. Not to be the idol, to have an aim of our own, there lies the truer pride, if we intend respect of ourselves.

The Mr. Pulpit young men have in them, until their habits have fretted him out, was directing Lord Fleetwood's meditations upon the errors of the general man, as a cover for lateral references to his hitherto erratic career: not much worse than a swerving from the right line, which now seemed the desirable road for him, and had previously seemed so stale, so repulsive. He was, of course, only half-conscious of his pulpitizing; he fancied the serious vein of his thoughts attributable to a tumbled night. Nevertheless, he had the question whether that woman— poor girl!—was influencing his thoughts. For in a moment, the very word 'respect' pitched him upon her character; to see it a character that emerged beneath obstacles, and overcame ridicule, won suffrages, won a reluctant husband's admiration, pricked him from distaste to what might really be taste for her companionship, or something more alarming to contemplate in the possibilities,—thirst for it. He was driving away, and he longed to turn back. He did respect her character: a character angular as her features were, and similarly harmonious, splendid in action.

Respect seems a coolish form of tribute from a man who admires. He had to say that he did not vastly respect beautiful women. Have they all the poetry? Know them well, and where is it?

The pupil of Gower Woodseer asked himself to specify the poetry of woman. She is weak and inferior, but she has it; civilized men acknowledge it; and it is independent, or may be beside her gift of beauty. She has more of it than we have. Then name it.

Well, the flowers of the field are frail things. Pluck one, and you have in your hand the frailest of things. But reach through the charm of colour and the tale of its beneficence in frailty to the poetry of the flower, and secret of the myriad stars will fail to tell you more than does that poetry of your little flower. Lord Feltre, at the heels of St. Francis, agrees in that.

Well, then, much so with the flowers of the two hands and feet. We do homage to those ungathered, and reserve our supremacy; the gathered, no longer courted, are the test of men. When the embraced woman breathes respect into us, she wings a beast. We have from her the poetry of the tasted life; excelling any garden-gate or threshold lyrics called forth by purest early bloom. Respect for her person, for her bearing, for her character that is in the sum a beauty plastic to the civilized young man's needs and cravings, as queenly physical loveliness has never so fully been to him along the walks of life, and as ideal worships cannot be for our nerving contentment. She brings us to the union of body and soul; as good as to say, earth and heaven. Secret of all human aspirations, the ripeness of the creeds, is there; and the passion for the woman desired has no poetry equalling that of the embraced respected woman.

Something of this went reeling through Fleetwood; positively to this end; accompanied the while with flashes of Carinthia, her figure across the varied scenes. Ridicule vanished. Could it ever have existed? If London had witnessed the scene down in Wales, London never again would laugh at the Whitechapel Countess.

He laughed amicably at himself for the citizen sobriety of these views, on the part of a nobleman whose airy pleasure it had been to flout your sober citizens, with their toad-at-the-hop notions, their walled conceptions, their drab propriety; and felt a petted familiar within him dub all pulpitizing, poetizing drivellers with one of those detested titles, invented by the English as a corrective of their maladies or the excesses of their higher moods. But, reflection telling him that he had done injury to Carinthia—had inflicted the sorest of the wounds a young woman a new bride can endure, he nodded acquiescence to the charge of misbehaviour, and muzzled the cynic.

As a consequence, the truisms flooded him and he lost his guard against our native prosiness. Must we be prosy if we are profoundly, uncynically sincere? Do but listen to the stuff we are maundering! Extracts of poetry, if one could hit upon the right, would serve for a relief and a lift when we are in this ditch of the serious vein. Gower Woodseer would have any number handy to spout. Or Felter:—your convinced and fervent Catholic has quotations of images and Latin hymns to his Madonna or one of his Catherines, by the dozen, to suit an enthusiastic fit of the worship of some fair woman, and elude the prosy in commending her. Feltre is enviable there. As he says, it is natural to worship, and only the Catholics can prostrate themselves with dignity. That is matter for thought. Stir us to the depths, it will be found that we are poor soupy stuff. For estimable language, and the preservation of self-respect in prostration, we want ritual, ceremonial elevation of the visible object for the soul's adoring through the eye. So may we escape our foul or empty selves.

Lord Feltre seemed to Fleetwood at the moment a more serviceable friend than Gower Woodseer preaching 'Nature'—an abstraction, not inspiring to the devout poetic or giving us the tongue above our native prosy. He was raised and refreshed by recollected lines of a Gregorian chant he and Feltre had heard together under the roof of that Alpine monastery.

The Dame collapses. There is little doubt of her having the world to back her in protest against all fine filmy work of the exploration of a young man's intricacies or cavities. Let her not forget the fact she has frequently impressed upon us, that he was 'the very wealthiest nobleman of his time,' instructive to touch inside as well as out. He had his share of brains, too. And also she should be mindful of an alteration of English taste likely of occurrence in the remote posterity she vows she is for addressing after she has exhausted our present hungry generation. The posterity signified will, it is calculable, it is next to certain, have studied a developed human nature so far as to know the composition of it a not unequal mixture of the philosophic and the romantic, and that credible realism is to be produced solely by an involvement of those two elements. Or else, she may be sure, her story once out of the mouth, goes off dead as the spirits of a vapour that has performed the stroke of energy. She holds a surprising event in the history of 'the wealthiest nobleman of his time,' and she would launch it upon readers unprepared, with the reference to our mysterious and unfathomable nature for an explanation of the stunning crack on the skull.

This may do now. It will not do ten centuries hence. For the English, too, are a changeable people in the sight of ulterior Time.

One of the good pieces of work Lord Fleetwood could suppose he had performed was recalled to him near the turning to his mews by the handsome Piccadilly fruit-shop. He jumped to the pavement, merely to gratify. Sarah Winch with a word of Madge; and being emotional just then, he spoke of Lady Fleetwood's attachment to Madge; and he looked at Sarah straight, he dropped his voice: 'She said, you remember, you were sisters to her.'

Sarah remembered that he had spoken of it before. Two brilliant drops from the deepest of woman's ready well stood in her eyes.

He carried the light of them away. They were such pure jewels of tribute to the Carinthia now seen by him as worshipping souls of devotees offer to their Madonna for her most glorious adornment.